Me Us And Them

Alycia Marie

Published by Alycia Marie, 2023.

This is a work of fiction. Similarities to real people, places, or events are entirely coincidental.

ME US AND THEM

First edition. September 9, 2023.

ISBN: 979-8224963119

Written by Alycia Marie.

Proluge

Good morning, America 20 years into the war it's now over. How much pain so much heartache so many lights are ruined so many kids gone to war. How many parents lost on 9/11 and I say again good morning, America.Stay tuned this just coming in repeating good morning, Vietnam stay tuned for breaking news as Robin Williams said good morning, Vietnam good morning, Afghanistan. It isn't even August 31st and yet here we are August 30th one day ahead but no they never said August 31st Afghanistan time. Like this is groundhog's Day but it's not. Like I've been through this before. I mean this has been going on since I was 15 30 plus years. My heart's broken just a little bit and sad and scared. For all those Americans left behind fighting for their lives in Afghanistan today. For them to get out. Maybe it's because my grandparents were in the military or because of the CVS I knew who fought in Iraq and Afghanistan and help build up the country by their own sweat and blood as they built playgrounds and basketball courts as I sent candy to them, and got in fights over Reese's pieces.

What happened to all those basketball courts now and all those dreams those kids had of being the next Superstar and all the girls are they even there or are they they training to take down Americans on those courts.Or maybe that's just who I am a sensitive gal who feels the pain in the loss of something big.

This is it turning point and I cried just a little in hearing the story of the Afghanistan who had his phone broken and beat up in the Americans who can't get out of the country and told they can't guarantee safe passage to the airport, sort of puts everything in perspective. Losing a kitty feels a little less important than fighting for your life.Right. I wonder if my niece will see history repeating itself too. Like it's a time loop, like all we have is time loops repeating and you can't get past the loop or are we in The matrix and all this is just fake. All the vets who fought in Afghanistan, thank you for the bottom of my heart sleep well tonight, folks you never know but tomorrow will bring, safe and prayers to those just trying to figure this out, what's next and are we on a break, there was breaks in between and yeah they were on a break right we can say that with the laugh and a giggle but guess what, not really they weren't on a break no sir.

And we destroyed that country and we left it and we are responsible for what happened. We should have stayed. Top commanders you know and rotate out or something but thank God the Russians are still there, that was God's plan don't you know. The Russians are coming maybe they'll be more scared of the Russians. I just don't know but I do know this yeah they were on a break in Afghanistan like for a few years and they can do whatever they want when they're on a freaking break but still we don't deserve to destroy a country on a break, I guess we're on a break again just a temporary break. We will see what happens on this break because their country is a mess. Thing is for sure Starbucks will close McDonald's will close do they even eat...just kidding. I Know the difference between Iraq and Afghanistan like that country song . Can we be serious just for a second my heart's broken I've said it before and I'll say it again my little heart is broken. Where were you when the world stopped turning to quote another country song and yes I do know the difference between Iraq and Afghanistan and yes I love country.

I'm not the typical country girl though so whatever on that but where were you seriously when the world stopped turning. I want to know. I was at home working from home because of covid my life had changed completely and of course I remember when the world stopped turning on 9/11 almost 20 years ago. Those kids did not have to die though I mean they were 20 one of them had a kid of his own they should not have died they didn't even know what 9/11 was did they? Give their freedom so that peace could be had by all. So Afghanistan's could get out , hopefully a few babies could get out because of them and didn't get trampled you know. I don't mean to be vulgar but I mean it does look like a rock concert and all those people but it's not and they aren't fans. It's For freedom. I don't think you can put Western values on them yeah clear out the Starbucks clear out the McDonald's. I know they're cheering in the street hip hip hooray the Americans are gone but they got another thing coming the Russians are there the Russians are there and who would have thought we would be celebrating that the Russians are there. I bet you never thought to say praise God thank you the Russians are there and thank you God for all the brave Americans that stayed behind and hopefully there are few going through tunnels as I write

this. Learned this as I watch Fox. Yes they are creating tunnels to get the Afghans and Americans out.

Just the average American citizens, will not average, military average well not even military average as they came when they were told not to so thank you Oliver North ,As Americans come they come as Americans have dueling presidents American president Trump and American President Biden one checking his watch as 13 soldiers died and one telling the world I would have done it different. Sending Afghans to Texas and Virginia Republican states to make

Democrats only time will tell what will happen. Culture shock for the women and men a Starbucks on every corner and women are free to be who they want to be. Yes only time will tell how this will all play out meanwhile Mexicans are working Afghanistans in another twist to the border wars. Just saying they were not on the break even if they took a little break here and there ask yourself if they get settled as a break good or not are we on a break. Afghanistan's can watch countless episodes of friends and learn English and maybe even countless episodes of Seinfeld or cheers.

. Yeah happy 9/11 day is that even a day ,if it's not it should be so we can remember the red bandana man who risked his life and remember the 13 who died to end the war so we will never forget. God even if you're not religious stand up praise God don't kneel say hip hip on 9/ 11 and we can order as many Starbucks frappuccinos as we want. For freedom. The way why is it 911 to Holiday I guess because we don't want it commercialized I guess you can just see it now it would be just another day get your free car get a discounted car and just another day to get drunk.I guess it's better for it not to be a holiday so we can be serious and remember I'm just saying with the wink and a smile and a nod Good morning America

JIMMY JR

Tim died, daddy to me died. but he got to see me play soccer professionally which was good. Now after we laid daddy Tim to rest. I went back there and kicked in some soccer but. Being the youngest was tough underdog kind of pressure on me and especially not knowing my dad that was tough but not that anyone expected me to be, but I was a kid that was born on 9/11 you know, and I was the happiness kid. That's how I felt anyway no one told me. I never felt that sadness like my brother says he's felt. The only thing hard is not knowing. My brother went to war, and he said he never had that anger he just had that responsibility to make a difference. I didn't really feel that. I don't know I didn't feel that responsibility or anger or sadness. I just wanted to live you know. That was how I felt. We are just living life. I guess we were that 9/11 family and to be that family it just felt normal but I mean I always wondered what if what would be different if he had lived but I really think about it and I think of not knowing Tim or Jen and then I get sad so I try not to think about it because I'm so bonded with Jen .I can't imagine not having a big sister and I mean Dylan might not even have gone to war you know I mean what would he have been doing. What would I have been doing not to be disloyal, but I could have been stuck playing football instead of soccer or working in business and I don't know if I wanted any of that. But would I have given that up. Just to know my daddy Jim yeah, I mean how can you say no how can you, you can't you just can't. I guess that's the hardest part, so I really don't think about that this much. I just think of it every now and then every time an anniversary comes about, and you push it aside and it's not out of guilt or at a fear it's because you want to live.

I know my dad would have felt that same way he would have just lived he'd understand, and I know he told me kiddo just live don't look back. It's true mom told me that all the time, he always just moved forward and so I take that advice from him, and I know he's smiling down from heaven this 9/11 , 20 years later. Twenty years is a long time. I got involved with the work I do now, and it became who I am because it was so important to keep being you and to try to make a difference. Which I feel like I did I feel lucky to be able to and really make a difference. I feel blessed to be able to play. it's important on all levels and to just have a blessed life. I'm not I mean I know I went through a lot as a kid, and I know sometimes my mom wasn't available, but I never felt sad. I felt like I pushed myself. I pushed myself to get things done and to be the person that I thought I could be, and I am told my dad, daddy Jimmy was like that, he really pushed himself when he knew he wanted something, he got it done but the same time that's how Tim was too but just in a quiet way nonaggressive way. So, I don't know who I take after. I guess the saying DNA versus nurture is what this is all about. Tim was there for all the firsts. I mean I don't remember but mum says he was there, and I learned how to walk and talk, and he helped potty train and he would take me for walks and then when I was old enough to remember Tim was there for me. I remember the first day of kindergarten and I know it couldn't have been easy for him sitting in the background on 9/11 hearing me and Dylan talk about the other dad but he didn't act like it and the fact that he was a fireman too he knew he knew .But it was like we had a piece of our dad they were both survivors in their own right. Mom knew him and then they just met at the firefighter friends of the firefighter building. She was going for support, and they were talking, and he was always just their. Mom says nothing really happened for ten years. I think if you asked him, he felt guilty for being. He would never admit it. He lost his wife who worked at 9/11 at the World Trade Center but I mean that's why this is so hard now and here we are 20 years later and Tim's not even around I mean I got jipped twice and I hate to say it like that but it's true.

Looking back on it all now I feel so sad it's not depression. I feel like very blessed. Now today I have two names to honor but I feel blessed because I truly got to know what love was .I fully understand the meaning of love. I have so many memories to fill my brain and then I have the memory the what if a parallel universe . If you will but like I said I don't go there today it's easy to slip. I cry' because I know all the stories and all the faces I just want to be loving. I just want life to be happy and not mean. That's who I am. I keep trying I always do. I wish Tim were here I do. I know he'd like all this pomp and circumstance and he always knew what to say unlike me. I was that kid that's always just quiet. I guess I will be I will be or keep it light, but they always say keep it quiet keep it real be strong. Tim always kept it real and strong I know I get that attitude from him interestingly. I'm just me though. I don't take anything for granted, I am grateful.

I don't know , I knew that Tim wasn't my real dad. I was already bonded with him when I knew. There's a father figure and a father and Tim was a father. So that's why when he got sick. I was there for him every way possible. Everyone could just help them out. I would have given up everything. Mom called me, it was so sad, I couldn't even believe it, but it was real, and it was hard to reckon with, I think. I was the baby of the family I was the one everyone took care of. I'm just trying to become my own person. I think I'm like challenging the status quo. This is going to be my story from start to finish I'm going to tell the truth and nothing, but the truth they say I don't have anything to hide... I'm going to tell what made me. I'm going to take the mystery out of it and who I am going to be. A big deal does, who is the 9/11 boy. I can see it now, if it was the old days, it would be like a circus freak show really, but it isn't and I'm not so yes to start off with I really was born on 9/11. I was born in a Brooklyn hospital my mom and nursed me in the hospital and daddy Jimmy of course was not there. I never knew him I didn't really feel lacking. I mean how can I. When you're just a newborn but I was secure kid even at one and two right I might add. Great kid though I'm not Tooting my own horn, but mom told me you could hold me for hours and I was just a quiet little kid.

I got to believe this because when I was older I remember being more secure and quiet I've always been quiet ,so I know Tim was telling the truth .It's funny if I have a question about myself I'll go to Tim and he knows everything my mom I mean yeah she was checked out I mean you can't blame her and I'm not mad at her and I feel really secure with who I am in life. So, I think that means from the child development classes. I've taken the psychology classes; this really means that I had a secure childhood. My first two years were good, I mean how can this be you ask if the world was in distress . My mother didn't care at first but I mean I know I was loved 100%. Because I didn't know better you see Dylan will be the first to say and so will Jen that they both feel like something was torn apart and I see kids who lost their dad at 7 or 8 and they always feel like a little piece of them is missing and that makes sense but at the same time they're secure because the first few years were good. But still to have that all taken away no wonder they feel a little sad , I don't know how it all works but maybe if you're one and you were kidnapped you might just feel the chaos. You know but even then, I mean the way I feel is they might have loved you, so you felt secure but then you question it all later that's what I'm thinking you know. I mean do I ever wish I was different., I can't say that. I really can't. I don't know when I've said it before but I'm going to say it again, you can't miss something you don't have. I miss the knowledge of him. I wish I could have multiple versions of myself and I know in a different reality the thing that comforts me is that another reality Jimmy never died .Jimmy never went on to work ,he never went to work that day and so he was there to go into labor and had he known that my mom was in labor. I don't think he would have went into work and just feel like as she tells it that she went into labor after he was gone. She was asleep and maybe it was a stress of everything that put her into false labor' cause she tried to call him and then of course it was too late he couldn't come back and she thought I'll get him to come back but he couldn't but as I said the only thing that really makes me happy is knowing in another reality I have my Jimmy I have my daddy or I think about cloning myself I think of cloning Jim, Jimmy taking some of his hair and creating another version of daddy Jimmy. So I could have him there too for the time that Tim wasn't there or if I had a time machine . I think that if I had a time machine I would I go back and tell my dad you're going to die if you go to work, now if you go to work you're going to die and I think to myself if I told him that what would happen well what would have happened. I mean maybe someone else would have died or someone else would have never been saved. I'm sure my dad would be fine but other people would have died instead or someone that he talked to. My dad died and I know I wouldn't want to change that cause he was an influential person. I know he helped other people and he did call. Mom said he did call people. He was so high he tried to warn people, but they couldn't get out. He was that high up I hate to think that he was that high up and I often wonder. HOW he helped people. Mom said he was a trained volunteer fire fighter. So, he knows what to do, that helps mom a lot. Thinking he was there to help others. Back to The Time Machine I don't know I guess I wouldn't do a time machine but I would like to clone him so I could have him just take a bunch of his hair. I wanted to be a scientist when I was in 8th grade for that very reason, I was thinking about taking some of those clothes mom still had cloning him, so I could see him and get to know him and hear his laugh cause the videos weren't enough or just going back in time for a minute. I created a whole dream sequence maybe I will get to tell my dad that I loved him. More than anything a thank you for creating me that's the one thing I would tell him. You know the touching dream sequence in a movie. A movie about that I mean I don't know my brother is a writer maybe he'll write a movie about that going back in time and saving your dad. I mean he should do it and Tim says cloning for sure. But I'll leave the writing to my brother, to Focus on my on my darker side.

Getting good at soccer... I mean I'm always deprived. I was the athletic one I mean. I know I do look like him. Dylan tried, and he did play football. I don't know maybe it's just because he wasn't that good. He was good enough, but we always joked about him that he would just fall for no reason, so he does take after mom a little bit on that note. I want to focus more on different realities because I think it's important it's not really cloning it's more for every reality there's something that you didn't do and that you did do. OK so for every decision you make there's another version of you so if my dad didn't go to work then that's one reality. There's another reality where he died but then on the way to work he had another chance maybe he missed the bus then then he got moms call before he went into the office so maybe he made it all the way there you know or maybe mom went into labor before you know that night and then and I got to meet him at least he got to hold me you know and then he had to go into work I like that one. I know it's dark but it's sticks for closest to the reality so whatever else was going to happen would have happened so I'm not being totally selfish cause I don't like to think of myself as a total selfish person you know so that's what I would have liked to happen just once from my dad to hold me and kiss me and have that photo but as it is I just think of that memory and in my mind sometimes to get through rough times. That's what I like to feel happened, but I know that it was Tim who hold me a couple days later that I have a picture

In my dreams which scares me sometimes I'll be dreaming of daddy Jimmy and then suddenly,of so at least I have a dad figure. I mean it wasn't like oh this is your dad and give him a Father's

he turns into Tim. I'm like no come back daddy but he does not, and I used to wake up screamingDay card but later yeah it was. Years later ten years later. I was like oh thanks dad and so I did that doesn't really happen anymore. I just have a little bit of sadness maybe that goes away withhave I did call him dad later. time too. I don't know I hope so but then again sometimes I don't want it to go away at all' because

I want to remember. I want to feel him want to feel the love with the pain. I don't want to forget all that I just can't. One question a lot of people ask me is do you mind that your mom got remarried. I am like no I want my mom to be happy and I guess that's another sign that I'm adjusted well. I will I want her to be adjusted well. I went off to college or if I went to different things that I wouldn't have to worry about her and I wanted ... I wanted that freedom and I wanted her to be happy of course I want to be happy of course I did .I guess Dylan did too but I think I don't want to tell you what I think Dylan's moment would be I think Dylan would choose and I'm not saying this because I think he's selfish but I think Dylan in my opinion would choose to never lose him so not to feel that pain .I don't know why I feel that way I mean maybe because that's what I would choose if I was if I was sad. If I was in my own sad place and if I had known my dad just for like 10 minutes how could you even give that up you'd want more so if I had my dad to hold me I would say oh well let me just spend a few days with him and then take him away and then it turned into a year then just give me six months more than just give me a year and then all of a sudden no never mind... I can't give him up at all. You couldn't so I guess that's why I feel that way or maybe Dylan would just want another 5 minutes with him.

I've asked him that and he just gets a sad look in his face he won't talk about it to me like I said I'm the more talkative one and freer about my emotions. You think I want to be more secure but that I would have more anxiety but by the time I was old enough mum had her life together and she had Tim, and everything was good it took 10 years and Dylan was already 16 at this time so he didn't have the benefit of all the good. He went along he had all the negativity years just doing his own thing that's why I think he's bit of a loner and why he had to go to war. I don't know if that's fair. I take it back about my brother I don't know if it's fair about Dylan. I do know though Tim gave him the ability to be a writer from what I know of daddy Jimmy he would have said OKAY but... and I think it's just not in his wheelhouse of things he would have been stuck being a PE teacher or you know, and I don't think he would have liked that too much. I don't know about Jen. Jen would have just been going back and forth too much. I don't know what she would have changed I know that Tim was divorced and so there's that, so I guess Jen has never said... if she wishes her mom lived. she knows how difficult it would have been, but I know she does wish she would have lived but I know she knew it was a tricky thing. It is just a totally tricky thing, makes you sad just thinking about it so I don't think about these things very often I'm just reenacting it now for you, so you know where I'm at. I just want everyone to know where I'm at and what I'm doing and who I am .I think it's important 'because I don't want to be seen just as the 9/11 kid. I'm over that as I grow up, I want what I do to be important, and I know it is and I know it will be. I mean it is now so I'm happy truly I am and I'm not just saying that. Super excited to see what my future is going to hold. I mean I feel like I'll get married I'll have kids and do all that stuff. That's just the way it is the girls will always be with you haunting your everyday. How can that not be the case it can't, so I've grown to accept it and live with it it's not a bad thing it just is. and it's not a bad thing it just is. They all stay with you they are a part of you just expect it. Knowing the way, the world is I won't be surprised if something else rocks the world I can see it but until then I do hope I can live a tiny bit of happily ever after if that truly exists as I say a tiny bit' because I don't believe happily ever after truly exists how can you. But I will tell you this they truly stay with you the ghosts my daddy Jimmy is always with me I see him wherever I go if you ask any 9/11 kid, they'll say the same their dads with them or their moms with them. Now even Tim is with me. He walks with me. It's just a pure fact so there that and there's nothing you can do about it. I think of it like they're there to guide you to do the right thing. How can this not be the case. I know my mom thought that, so I do too but it's a reality it's not just something then we made up, like I said you ask anyone about this, and they'll say the same thing. I could just plain read the book and maybe we wanted to seem that way, but I know it's true not just fantasy they're there

It's not that I didn't want to be like him you know. I love my dad it's just sometimes it gets too much I didn't want to be the 9/11 kid. I didn't want to be on any of that I really didn't but at the same time I was honored. I'm glad that Mom saw a lot of him and me I really am and now I agree with Mom then I couldn't. But I really do see that Dylan bless his little heart, was more like Mom and I was like him but at the same time I'm a lot like Tim too there's a lot to be said about nurture. I'm strong like him and I got that go get so attitude. I don't think Jimmy had that. Daddy Jimmy had that, but I got the love of sports that's for sure and I know he'd be proud of me. As for Dylan as much as doing when the play sports. It was good for high school but that was about it he was never going to go beyond that and doing it too it was just having fun but even him he got to be something different because of Tim maybe he would have been a coach and hated it I don't know from a distance I can see that maybe daddy Jimmy didn't like his job, but you never know Present

JEN

Fog, fire, chaos, and loud noise that is what our childhood was all about. Oh, and loss. Always loss in the background. Making you who are. Challenging you to get beyond it but you can't do that. You can never forget that loss that forms who you are, who you became. Losing a parent is always hard but, but on such a huge scale its even harder. You look for that little bit of light to guide you from the darkness, you take what you can. I listen on September 11 and hear the bells toll as they say they the names of those we lost and I remember my dad and listen for his name and then Kathy and Jens mom . They will never be forgotten.

I often wonder though what would have been different If my dad had lived. Who would I have become if he lived? What if ...Happily ever after. But then I think of not knowing dyl or Tim ...then what if again. No, we will never forget those people that died on that September morning, you know just people living out their everyday routine, not knowing that this was the end. That they would never know their unborn son but thinking and dreaming of their future. I cry because there is no rewind button and even if there was would I, could I, give up the only dad I knew? What if...what if...! This is our story; this is the story of how we became a family. It all started that morning at Grand Central station.

I say it's a story of a family, but I realize it's more than that it's a story of how a city and little towns became a family. We all took care of ourselves and others around us that's the way it was and that's what makes me happy. There are pictures of people all over the building somewhere on the ground some are blowing in the wind there was flowers and words that say I love you, call if you can, we miss you, come home. I will never forget those people on that September morning twenty years ago. How can we when the images stay with us through life and the children we see, through going to the airport and just living, but we do not let them win. We live, we live for all those who we lost and to just live. We will always remember those who died and those who were trying to save those from dying. They are people just living everyday lives. What if... And here we are. We were destined to end up together nearly twenty years ago. Our destinies became intertwined after that faithful September morning. They stay with us and watch and help and guide us through all the difficult times. Proud that we became family and they watch.

One day Angela calls me saying dad is sick get home and we all do . Dylan, me and Jimmy Jr rush home to be there for him.

When I get the call to rush home I'm in Los Angeles. I have a few comedy gigs lined up. Before I have to make my next film but I drop it off to rush home to see I have no choice I have to. I'm on the first flight. To the airport and I sit there a few hours but it doesn't matter. I pray and I think about all the things that I've done with him. All the memories and I pray that he's okay. That I have time to say goodbye. I love you Daddy I whisper and tell him to hold on.. I curse that he had to get this disease but there's nothing that can be done. He did so much he was a hero.

He is a first responder hero from 9/11 and he's been there for us as long as we all remember of course. No he didn't die on that September morning but he's a first responder and hero non the less. No it took him 20 years for that to happen. I never really ends. Those hijackers in that plane they continue to do us in after all this time. Why they say you'll never forget because it goes on and on you know with covid-19 the first responders from 9/11 are getting it the covid yeah and so it continues. Because they all had preconditions but I'm not here to talk about that. But these are the thoughts that are going through my head as I wait for the plane. As I board the plane, as I Rush to my mom's house , I think If those guys weren't dead I'd want to kill them again. I try to think of something funny to cheer myself up but it doesn't work not today. Today going right back to my teen angst self . How can I not. Everything from that day comes rushing in. When I get on the plane I take anxiety pills and put my headphones on and cover up my eyes . After silent prayer for nothing to happen the plane. I always do this when I fly. I don't always fly if I can avoid it I will, but I can't today, I have to get home as fast as I can. As soon as I get home I run and find Mama and hug her .

Angela's sad of course and wonders why this happens to her. Why she loses the love of her life after everything they've been through and now, she's lost the love of her life twice. But she has them, she has us kids... who keep us to keep her strong and well.

I am a comedian and when I perform comedy, I tell everyone there is ghosts watching us doing everything including taking a piss...that usually gets a big belly laugh. But it's true the ghosts are among us, watching our every move and we can go to the past and talk to them any time we want

.

Dylan

Yes I was five years old when my first dad died. I tried to make it like a sitcom but that's what I needed back then. All I could do to cope. I'm from Brook But I live in New York City now and I write twenty years later, and I still remember that day people say how can you remember well I was just a kid. I know that but it was intense all said and I became the man of the house and only eight years old I had to take over my dad and I were really close he was more everything we play for hours my mom can vouch for that I am very close to daddy Tim don't get me wrong but it took me years years to get there to really appreciate him mom says I fell asleep in my helmet all the time I would sleep in it I'd wake up crying I vaguely remember that and I remember doing that for months. I still think of what my dad would have wanted, and I try to be that better person I really feel like I must be that perfect person just to honor my dad's memory. I know no one really expected that from me still that's what I do death would I feel like I must do um I don't like doing it, but I do I try my hardest to not shake things up I put a lot of pressure on you sometimes and then all my counseling I've learned finally to just be myself and that's the hardest thing. When I was fifteen, I was busy finding my identity, trying to fit in. In high school I was full of angst. Looking back couldn't have been too healthy. I decided that at eighteen to go fight the war I knew yeah of course they'd already got Bin Laden, but I had to go I had to do it I was praying I would get sent to Afghanistan. And so, at eighteen I went to the marines. I really did not ask my mom and Tim's permission. Just told them money for school and I know we didn't have a lot of it, and I told him that Jimmy would be looking out for me that daddy Jimmy would be there for me. That won mom over and Tim he said he is proud of me, and he was sure that my dad would be too, so I did it. I was ready I want to boot camp and I passed with flying colors, and I was in and sure enough I got sent to Iraq. Yeah, it was nothing, but I thought it would be like, but it was hello on wheels to be exact, but I killed OK I literally killed, but it was worth it I got to feel like I was doing something. When some someone always said you look like your dad you have his personality and so on and part of the reason why I did this I just had to go to make my dad proud to find a part of myself and just to make myself feel better. I know they were worried, but I had to do it. Life was hard growing up and I know Tim was doing his best. I know it's happy for my mom and I grew to love him and do not get me wrong I mean looking back now I know he's all I knew, and I know we're close and I couldn't imagine life without him but.... Yeah, there was times that I got the fight where he told me do this do that and I would yell bloody murder you're not my father. Typical teen angst right. I was like FU leave me the F alone and I would storm up to my room. I just run away. I play my music loud and I would just annoy the F out of everybody but it made me feel good and of course later on I would come downstairs and I apologized to and Tim would say family as is never saying you never have to say you're sorry and I would hug him and smile .You know sometimes I would just stare at the photo of my dad Jimmy saying why daddy why you had to leave, I miss you so much you know and I would tell him everything I did and I know he would listen to me and I had imagined everything that he said telling me that he was proud of me and that I did the right thing and don't listen to anyone you're the best smartest boy in the whole world.

There's only so much I could do looking back now but back then I don't think I knew it.

Now I want to be there for mom and Jimmy. I'm glad I knew my dad jimmy. Late night I would still look at pictures from the photo albums. I would go up into the attic and just look at all the albums' moms had. I would even grab a video and put it on the VCR, so I won't forget what he looked like and at times even let Jimmy get involved. I felt like it was important for him to know what dad was like. And mom was too busy, so I was It. Me and Jimmy bond over daddy Jimmy which is good and I think it did save him it was important for him to know and be in touch with his emotions and later when mom found out that I showed Jimmy the videos she was surprised but very glad that I did and of course that was looking back but at the time I'm just doing it with no real intended purpose but the older me is glad that I did but still that does not change the fact that high school was a bit of a disaster and was a sports guy so I sort of felt like I have to play sports I had to be that guy. There was a legacy and then we grew up in a small town in jersey. Dad commuted to the World Trade Center. 9/11 you can look across the water and see the towers, but they even called Tim because he is a fighter fighter. They needed all the help, they could get. I guess he was back up not that they did do a good job. You know just talking about it all makes it feel so weird it was intense but anyway I was in like the marines for like five years. Not much to say I will say it was the most intense time in my life being in the military and though the family is all proud of me and Jimmy did his job he was protecting me no complaints here or from my family. I know they all think. He watched over me and who am I to contradict it. Right? Oh, I just focused on doing my best in school and helping everybody. I was after all the Big Brother and then you add a girl to the mix like Jen, so it got complicated. I feel like I became like a bad boy in high school, music and cool things but me, but I guess through all that teen angst it was worth it because here I am now super strong, and I will get everything I want and make a real difference which is great. I'm not thinking about it. I guess in high school and joining the marines right after high school. It was a way just to get out. It wasn't that everything was too perfect it just was, I guess they said it and I'll say it again I just needed to find myself which I did that's why I'm back and trying to get a little bit of closure. Hey everyone needs that, I think I had to go to fight in the war in Afghanistan because it's my way of Saying you took my dad away and I'm going to get you for that f u .And so I thought I was over there two tours intense man I'm not going to lie and I guess I really did think it would relieve some anxieties by going over there I don't want to get emotional but when I got out I was not the same person I was when I went and not just because I killed people .I don't have any of that teen angst anymore. Sure, I remembered my dad all the time darling daddy Jimmy, but I sure did remember him of course and I will not let any of that go I couldn't how I. I found out who I was apart from my family. I guess anyone would really but for me it was an important step I got over my anxiety of flying um I was able to open about my emotions. I let it all hang out. I'm finding out who I was I think I finally got to be me and that was important. Always being compared to someone was hard and when I got back, I was so different people have a chance to see me for who I was and not who they wanted to me to be I'm not saying they all saw me. Was good to get away from all that and step out and that really did help. I was a very strong person and having known my dad even just for that little bit I was always asking myself what he would do, and I wanted to make him proud and so I never really got to be me, and I think that led to me being this Golden Boy in high school. Yeah, right now I got to goof off and no one knew I was just in number no one really cared about my history, or who I was I had a blank slate which is perfect. Me and my brother Jimmy are different. I'm very open and emotional and I think my brother is well let's just say he holds back a little bit I really feel like he does I'm always encouraging him to be stronger. Be more real take a chance, say how he feels but I know he must find himself even though he didn't know my dad. It is okay to miss him. I know that sounds weird how can you miss someone that you never knew but maybe you can miss knowing them. I think that's the key in for me I always think about all the things I would have done with him and that stop me from living completely.

I'm in New York when I get the news so I don't have too far to go. After college I moved back to

New York to be closer to home and to write and sing .It just felt like the right thing to do. New York always had my heart and soul. Since I don't have that far to go I am the first to arrive. But nonetheless I'm in a daze . I'm stopping all the way to the train station to Brooklyn and then I get on the wrong train , twice and I have to go back and forth and finally through my tears I managed to find myself at Mama's and Tim's door.

I too am seeing all the memories of everything we've done together and I want to get revenge on those bastards from 9/11. I know daddy was sick. Poor daddy Tim. I want, I've always wanted to get his stories instead of just just being a kid. I mean he had so many great stories about New York and the firefighters people need to hear. Especially about that day. Now it's almost too late. I hope I have time to really hear not that I'm going to pressure him for stories but daddy always like to talk about it. It probably helps him find some peace, to remember. Like most war heroes and that's what he was a war hero, the first of them. Daddy Tim liked to talk about them because it kept them alive. So I know I can get enough stories to cover a whole book to make sure he and the others live on. With this in my mind I managed to make it on the right train finally and after what feels like an eternity I knock and go right into Mom's and dad's house. Mom's in the attic and she's glad to see me. I hug her and ask about Dad and she said hanging in there. I'm not and I head to the bedroom and ask him if I can get him water dad tries to smile and whisper something, I lean in and I assume he's asking for water I get him his cup with a straw and he takes a sip and then pushes it away he says I can't believe it Dylan, I can't believe it's come to this. I nod and I sit down. He whispers softly. Telling stories about fires and what he saw that day and I make a mental note of it all and try to record all the stories in my mind. It seems like minutes but I know it's hours Jen and Jimmy Jr come in and we all sit around the coffee table in the living room telling stories as Daddy rests . I tell Mama I want to go and check on him and I slowly walk in and I see him talking to himself and I just stand there and watch and smile. Love you Daddy Tim.

TIM

I see his shadow by the door and I smile. I mumble something and look away from Dylan , not wanting him to see me in pain .Stay away from that, they're coming to get us, boys. I mumble that I got out just in time.I want to go back I needed to get more people. I just happened to be downstairs and I fell to the ground and a firefighter grabbed me and pulled me I said I want to go back in. I got to do it. The figure by the window nods and I get more aggravated. No you don't understand we have to do this. I have lost consciousness and I see it's going again. The moment of clear is leaving I smile at Dylan and hug him. And the clearness is gone and the fog is back. And all I hear as I cough the world trade center cough, as we call it ,is boom boom boom and I say do you hear that ,stop the noise stop the noise, we got to save them. Then it's quiet again and I sigh. It's like I'm there all over again, it's like it never ended. I want to explain to Dylan in my lucid moments everything that I did . But time is elusive.

Dylan

I too am seeing all the memories of everything we've done together and I want to get revenge on those bastards from 9/11. I know daddy was sick. Poor daddy Tim. I want, I've always wanted to get his stories instead of just just being a kid. I mean he had so many great stories about New York and the firefighters people need to hear. Especially about that day. Now it's almost too late. I hope I have time to really hear not that I'm going to pressure him for stories but daddy always like to talk about it. It probably helps him find some peace, to remember. Like most war heroes and that's what he was a war hero, the first of them. Daddy Tim liked to talk about them because it kept them alive. So I know I can get enough stories to cover a whole book to make sure he and the others live on. With this in my mind I managed to make it on the right train finally and after what feels like an eternity I knock and go right into Mom's and dad's house. Mom's in the attic and she's glad to see me. I hug her and ask about Dad and she said I'm hanging in there. I head to the bedroom and ask him if I can get him water dad tries to smile and whisper something, I lean in and I assume he's asking for water I get him his cup with a straw and he takes a sip and then pushes it away he says I can't believe it Dylan, I can't believe it's come to this. I nod and I sit down. He whispers softly. Telling stories about fires and what he saw that day and I make a mental note of it all and try to record all the stories in my mind. It seems like minutes but I know it's hours Jen and Jimmy Jr come in and we all sit around the coffee table in the living room telling stories as Daddy rests . I tell Mama I want to go and check on him and I slowly walk in and I see him talking to himself and I just stand there and watch and smile. Love you Daddy Tim.

Tim

It's like it never ended. I want to explain to Dylan in my lucid moments everything that happened. I never wanted to talk about it as much as I should but today I did. I Blurt out everything I saw that day. All the bodies falling in the smoke and all the emotions how it made me sad and want to cry. How we had to hold it together and we couldn't really cry, how we had to just get through it all and we did. The people I work with that day did not make it. Lucky or maybe I was unlucky but I have to believe I was lucky because I got to meet Dylan and Jimmy Jr and of course Angela at the same time how can you not have survivors guilt.

All the bodies falling in the smoke and all the emotions how it made me sad and want to cry. How we had to hold it together and we couldn't really cry, how we had to just get through it all and we did. The people I work with that day did not make it. Lucky or maybe I was unlucky but I have to believe I was lucky because I got to meet Dylan and Jimmy Jr and of course Angela at the same time how can you not have survivors guilt, though. Now I do get Misty and I grab a hold of Dylan and won't let him go and all the tears just well up like a waterfall, just fall from my eyes. Dementia from 9/11 from working in the pile. I don't know how bad it'll get. How much I'll remember. I told Angela If I get really bad please put me out of my misery. She will ,I know she will. I took all the tests a few years ago and they said it's odd for someone in their fifties to be having this much dementia they said other firefighters were taking the same test other police officers too and they all had the same problems so they knew what it was ,what the problem was. Just didn't know how much time there was left. I just appreciated the time I did have left and I'm glad the kids came to spend time with me,my final days would be with the kids and Angela that we would be all together. I close my eyes a little bit and I'm glad that Dylan is there finally as I wait for the other kids to come.

DYLAN

Daddy Tim closed his eyes and I watch him for a minute before I left and headed to the Attic because that's where I knew Mom would be. I was glad that I caught a moment of mindfulness as mom's called it. He goes in and out and I know that by me being there it helped him be aware and it gave him peace of mind. I closed the door and let him sleep.

Angela

While I'm waiting, I go to the Attic to look at the memories to keep my self sane. To find myself and deal with all the pain.i am remembering back to when it all happened to beginning. Right after it happened I would call them the hospital's I was putting up signs everywhere. Convinced how could I not be that he was coming back that he just had amnesia or something. But he didn't. I felt his presence that night in bed and I knew he was sitting there he told me he wasn't coming back stop looking . I cried how can I stop but he just touched me and said I love you. That was the first time I've many that I would talk with him. Is there for me and he continues to be there for me. I'm remembering all that as I go through this with Tim. Then I remember what Tim told me when I asked why is it that I out live all the love of my lives. He cried as he squeezed my hands and said because we wouldn't know what to do without you baby and she sits there and holds his hand and goes for tea and that's when it happens. She hears a scream and runs in and shouts I love you. One last breath. I love you, he whispers, tell the kids . It's not his time not yet though. And it isn't he has a little bit more left but he frowns and shakes his head and I said yes you're not going anywhere. He tells me to tell them that he loves them. I love him I say and that's when I call the kids, and they rush home. And that's where they found me, in the attic .Dlyan finds me first in the Attic looking through every newspaper clipping, every photo album crying on bated breath looking at pictures of Jimmy senior holding Dylan and seeing Jimmy Jr and his cap and gown and his prom. I cry where does time go. I can't Believe Jimmy is now twenty years old and playing football, well European football. but still... he knows daddy Jimmy would be proud. There is no rewind button.

JIMMY JR

Today is the day we will always remember. I never would have thought a few years ago I would be standing here during another tragedy.

I am playing soccer in LA when i get a call from Jen to come home. I yell to my teammates got to go my dad's sick and that's that. I didn't know my dad all I had was Tim. He was my dad by the time I realized he wasn't it didn't matter. I mean for all intents and purposes I had two dads one I didn't know and one I didn't know. Mom made sure I remembered that he had a picture of him up and I got to love him. But I wasn't the 9/11 kid. I didn't want to be that. My sister and brother kid me about it. Jen being the photographer and performer interviewed me several times when I started to play for the Galaxy about being the 9/11 kid.

I didn't care I wore it well he printed in her magazine that I was single in which I was but right now I didn't care about all that as I made my way on the airplane and passed the magazine that said I was single. I grabbed it up and put my earplugs in and fell asleep on the plane wondering what was going to happen. Dad was going to die. I was going to be alone again. I got tears in my eyes and I cried a little. I'm not going to lie sometimes I do feel robbed sometimes I feel like I don't know any better. I know I said I had two dads but still one I never knew and one that loved me like I was his own. I it was just ...I know it was tougher on Mom, but my sister was always kidding me about being a mama's boy when Jen called me, she said have you seen dad and I said no. I made it there though I made it there sooner than I thought . Dad hadn't passed yet. I got to sit with him and watch him. Dad told me I was a good boy squeezed my hand and told me I was a good boy and my sister came in with breakfast and we just sat and watched TV. The announcer says there was a fire on 26th Street. Tim got a look on his eye and said that's a bad part of town and I nodded and said yeah, and Dad thanked Jen for breakfast. Mom got into bed and sat next to him and smiles at all of us. Glad to have us all around. Dad asked me if I was going to beat those son of a b and I said yeah Dad and suddenly, he looked exhausted. We let him go, he took one last breath and that was it. I like to think he died thinking about the fire that was Dad's life. It was hard to believe it's been 20 years already.As I sat in the house I grew up in my mind is already starting to wander. I wonder back to my, my senior year, which was a very weird year and prom was the least of it. I mean most of our senior year was spent online. We did not know if we were going to walk down the so-called line for graduation or if we were going to have a drive-by as they called it and then prom was out of the question of course.

My generation sure got the shaft of it , gen z they call us. I don't mind our generation likes to joke that we got the worst of everything I know it seems like a bad joke but still how can you joke about it , how can you not joke about it. You still have to , I mean we had 9/11 we have covid maybe what's next? You name it we got it. Jen and Dylan had a perfect prom. When it comes to my prom our parents knew what to do, they created some cool parties just for a few of us and at least I had Kelly. I mean we did date a lot and we grow closer during covid. I mean we always dated off and on but during that year it was our year, and we went to our little prom where we had music and social distancing with a couple of other friends. Nothing stops us we're survivors you know. We had to be right there's no stopping us from doing what we want to do we can't let it stop us. Anyway, even if we wanted to, we are not quitters we can't be. So, we made the most out of everything and enjoyed our proms and of course graduation too. But as far as proms go it was the bomb, we couldn't have asked for anything more really. We are survivors. I think of this we are survivors my whole family is survivors. I've been through so much, we have been through so much. Then I close my eyes and I wonder what Daddy Jimmy would think. What are you done about prom and graduation. I know he would have been proud of me but I need to create a story I need to know what he would have done.

Jimmy Sr

I saw my son at prom I was the proudest dad. I gave him money for the limo and I winked at him. I knew that's what I would have wanted so I gave him that. I gave him what I wanted. I remembered what it was like to be young and I was proud. I wanted Jimmy to seize the moment . And seize the moment he did. I couldn't be more proud of him that night. Again I winked at him slipped him a little extra money when Angela wasn't looking and told him to have fun with his girl friend. He smiled and laughed . Then he left and I smiled at Angela who's a little Misty eyed and I put my arms around her and smiled and we kissed and we waited up on the couch all night. He came back around 2:00 a.m. and I wanted to carry him to his bed like when he was a toddler like I used to do. But instead I just said how was it . He told me and then we sat down on the couch and we talked for about an hour and I just listened to everything he had to say. I was just glad to be there. I was so proud of him. Proud and happy.

Jimmy Jr

I open my eyes and look around and then look at the ground. That is what I imagine would have happened, but not just imagine because I know my daddy Jimmy was around.He was around in spirit I know that. He may not have been there for prom but still I had him in my memory in my mind. Yeah he wasn't there but you know what makes it even stronger to sit there and imagine what and to know that in spirit he was even if you physically wasn't there.

No we will never forget names and heroes. We will never forget.

You know I often wonder what would've been different if my dad had lived. Like I said . Who would I become...who we would have been if she and him would've lived ...what if...happily ever after... then I think of not knowing Tim and dly...then what if... again...we will never forget those people on that morning that changed every thing, just people living every day lives but what if...then I cry because there is no rewind button? That's right no rewind buttons. And now I'm home. Home to the only dad I knew and now he too is passing. It seems so unfair. I only got twenty years with him and I want more. That day keeps ruining lives. I don't think it'll ever stop and for that I'm near tears. As I head into the house I wipe away the tears and trying to be strong but as soon as I see the house the flooded tears begins and I can't let it go. All the memories come back and they won't go away. This is the only family I knew and now the grieving starts all over again.

Tim

I'm glad the kids all came back. It makes me happy. Not that I thought that they wouldn't come back. They would it's just so happy to get one more time to be a family. Everyone smiles and cry tears one last time and as a dad I should comfort them and tell him it's okay. Seeing them all makes me remember when they were just little babies. And they smiled up at me and let them hear all the stories from when they were little . It's amazing how fast time goes when they smile up at me , all I see is at 15,13, 11, and all in that order. I'm glad they came, I'm glad I got to see them one last time and to tell them as much as I can about we all became a family and why it's so important for us to stick together. I know I'm going to cry a little bit but I have to I have to get it all out.

There's no regrets and if I could I do it all again, I have to . I know it doesn't make sense but even if I knew what was going to happen to me on that September Day, I'd still go in because I know I help people by going in and how could you not that's my job anyway that's what I'm supposed to do, and that's what I tell them all in a quiet weeping low energy voice. I told them just to live their lives so that you have no regrets that is what I've learned. That's what I know, that's what I hope they pass on to their kids someday and for them to remember about me and tell my story. I know they arec doing well . Jimmy's always been the writer and Jimmy the adventure and Jen my little angel the creative one ,though they are all the same so strong . They all get that from me I suppose . I'd like to think that anyway . I like to think I influenced the boys just as much as Jen and I know they would tell me that I did . I'm glad I could give a part of myself to them really I am. And I tell them that and yet another story in the low whisper. They are great kids you know and I know Angela knows. What a rough time they're going to have but I try not to think of that now. I let it all go so I can get the words out, so I can get the story out.We work so hard to become a family and we did it. Wasn't always easy but in the end the bond we created is unbreakable. Because it was our destiny. Out of the ashes and because of them we found each other and they comforted each other to become family.

Past

Angela

The first thing I remember about that morning is I was nine months pregnant and that September 11th it was 7:00 in the morning when I thought I was in labor. I almost wanted to call him, but I thought it'll be hours before I'm in labor and my water breaks and then hours before the baby even comes so I don't call him, I wish I had. Jimmy sr left that morning at 7:00 a.m. from our house in Brooklyn and if I called everything would have been different. I don't know why I didn't it's about the only thing I regret in this world. If you know me, I don't regret much but that I mean, how could I not regret it. Given what I know and Dylan and Jimmy jr would have had him as a father and I would have had him as a husband and then I realize I would have never known Tim or Jen. I know how I can trade a life for a life. I see Jimmy and I look back and a feeling of relief flashes over me. Does God know what he's doing. I don't know. I really don't know but I do know I get so confused so I must stop thinking of it and I just let life flow. All I remember is a lot of screaming and a lot of pain and I rushed to the hospital. I was wrong it was a relatively quick labor the doctor says because it's my second. Maybe. It's 8:40 in the morning and I want to call, and I do. It's too late I can't get through. When i gave birth to Jimmy I remember laying on the bed screaming. The nurses are crying, and the TVs are blaring but they try not to let me see it. The downstairs waiting room was empty no one's coming they had the blood ready, they had everything, and no one came but the nurses and doctors were all glad to be that day with a baby. In the baby part you know where at least one miracle could happen even though through their tears they were crying. There's only one baby born that day, which is strange, but everyone came to see Jimmy Jr when he was born, he was crying but he was a miracle baby. Someone even took his picture and that picture ended up in Time magazine labeling him the miracle baby Brooklyn that would haunt him forever. I screamed and cried but finally the baby pushed out and she held him tight, she watched the TV and watched Jimmy suck all it's okay baby. It's okay she said to Jimmy, and he held him tight your daddy can't wait to see you he's going to love you baby. Yes, he is, you're going to be loved and safe, yes you are, and she held them tighter, and she watched the TV screen. I didn't want to believe that he wasn't safe she wasn't even thinking of that. I tried to dial his number but no answer. I left him a message saying baby I had the baby call me when you get this i tried 20 times still no answer. I didn't know he was struggling for his life on the 60th floor. I didn't want to believe that. He had to be okay, he had this new life to take care of.

He looked like a movie star. Jimmy Sr was my first love. The father of my babies and if that day never happened, we would still be together. We were that couple. People ask how can you fall in love again then? If you found your soul mate. Yes, I found my soul mate, but I know Jimmy would have wanted me to be happy. I know it sounds like a movie right but it's true. What I felt for Jimmy or feel for Tim doesn't take away from the love I feel, felt. When I look at My baby I think of Jimmy. Jimmy Jr looks just like him, but he acts like Tim.

Where Dyl looks like me and acts like Jimmy. He has the same behavior and passions of Jimmy. But there is a bit of softness, I think he gets that from Tim, you know. Then there is Jen, she's the daughter I never had. I know she had a mom, but I get to be there for her and giggle with her like I can not with the boys. So, it's nice. The first time she crawled up on my lap I melted. It was hard for sure but over time you lose just a little bit of that pain and forget just a little bit. You never forget totally, how you can, but it sure helps to find a love that makes you whole again and brings a little joy back to your life. But still I still sit and hope that in another reality my husband lived . I can see it now . I'm happy that he's there for the birth of your baby and to help bring Jimmy Jr home. We are so happy .

JIM SR

I leave for work as usual. I peek at Dylan I grab a coffee and kiss my wife goodbye. Back for dinner I say. Nothing special nothing out of the ordinary just a normal Tuesday morning. I get to work around

8:00 after taking the train and sit down at my desk on the 100th floor and look at my window and work. I'm typing up on a story. I think I'm calling Angela, but I get sidetracked with work. And I think well she'd let me know if she was in labor, so I think about it I put my hand on the phone around 8:30 the time of the first blast and then of course it's too late. I do call later though to tell her I love her and not to worry we will be okay. I can't tell her the truth there's fire all around fire as far as I can see. I'm wondering if I can get out how I can get out. I try all the exits, but I don't find any that don't have fire I go to the windows it's too far down. And look at someone running towards the window and opening it I run to stop them but it's too late and I look out and it's getting smaller and smaller, and I see a female come flying by. I go to the window again and look down. I'm wondering if they maybe had a net. if I'll, be I called the fire department I try and tell them I'm stuck on the 100th floor I have a green shirt on. Can you get me out I asked the 911 operator, and she says they'll try? I said you guys have nets it's a long way down there be the only way to save us. she said she doesn't know but you'll find out. I looked down and just see dots on the ground it's too hard to tell. and I step back from the window. I won't do it. I'll take my chances at the at the stairs. Always been afraid of heights. I know a weird job huh, but I started like believing I was in the clouds, and I had to really to just float. I didn't look down much. No, the fire is getting warmer, and I must make a move. I look at the exit again and open the door and hurl myself down the stairs hoping that I'll get out, did I have a future then I'll see my wife and kids again.

TIM

I look out at my window in Brooklyn. I love Brooklyn, Brooklyn is the best place to be. I'm not just saying that because it's my hometown neither. Of course, I have allegiance to this place but nonetheless Brooklyn makes me feel happy and in the fall it's full of energy just a little bit chill after the long summer and you feel like anything is possible. That's difference between Brooklyn and New York City. Now you may ask what someone like me was doing at the world trade center if I'm from Brooklyn . Well I would say it's because they needed us Brooklyn kids in New York cuz we are the best of our bunch. That's our standard answer but no in reality just because we'd want to give everything we can and just go. I was just running late to work. But I still took my time to just slowly get ready. Before I go to work at 6:00 am and see my long day of work. I was expecting nothing amazing hopefully just to chill day at the firehouse, normally a good day is when you had to do nothing. Skies are already a little blue this chilly day, but you can tell it's going to be nice as I said and was imagining how I would play with Jen afterwards. After work maybe run through some leaves jump in piles of leaves with her. I was running a little late, so I didn't have much time to appreciate it, but I was in a hurry as usual. That morning I rushed to work I kissed my wife, and we were on the outs no one knew this, and I didn't tell anyone for years except for Angela finally. I couldn't tell him I was so sad as I should be I knew we were divorcing. I had the papers, but I kissed her nonetheless I must have known but I rushed out the door like it was a normal day. Kathy was dropping off Jen after at school and she was to pick her up and she had to work late and had a meeting little did I know then that I would not pick her up that my mother would. I imagine Kathy at her desk .I don't know if she knew Jim Sr. but later, I found out the Jim and her worked in the same floor . She never mentioned him, but it was a big building, but my mind wanders, and I like to think they did know each other it's a very small world. I know people think Kathy and I were a mismatch, and we were she was an office chick, and I was a firefighter, but I guess you like that I seem like I was a bad boy I gave her some excitement, but opposites do not always attract though, and funny Angela is a stay-at-home mom. I don't think her, and Jim would have divorced maybe our paths would have crossed if the kids were at a football game and I would have seen him during football season with Jen as a cheerleader but that would have been it. As it is our paths met because we were both in grief and supporting each other and fell in love, and we got many years together.

But that day I rushed to the world trade center. As I was on my way, I saw the fire truck in Brooklyn zooming by and I got there just in time as my truck was pulling out and I jumped on and we went into the city to help our brothers and sisters.

I tried to call Kathy and tell her to get out that day I tried to get to the 90th floor but something kept distracting me and I prayed to God that she got out, but I think somehow, I was avoiding because I knew I couldn't do the job. I like to think I also saw Jim I think , or like to believe I did , at one point rushing down the stairs rushing back and forth trying to help people. I am not sure, but I'd like to think it's true. I told him to stay but he wouldn't. I tell the story to Dylan and Jimmy Jr Jen and Jen asked if I saw mom and I said honey it was too far up, but you know she was helping guide people that's who she was. I'm a lot closer to Jen now than I would have been if they've got if we have gotten divorced would have been a weekend dad a weekend warrior, they call them. I'm glad that I had more of her I'm not glad that this happened just glad that I had more of her.

KATHY

As Tim said we were getting divorced. That morning on 9/11 it was just a typical morning. I had no idea it'd be the last time I saw my family. I was in a hurry as usual Tim left early for the firehouse and I was heading to the world trade center. I jumped in off to school and gave her a hug and said see you later kiddo. And that was that. Then I was at work. I was on the 50th floor. I tried to help people as much as I could. I gathered everybody from my floor and told him what to do it's the mother and me and then we went, and I was checking to make sure that everyone was gone. There's no more elevator and so I started walking. As I was walking, I prayed and said I love you to my daughter and to my husband. When I was little Mr. Rogers said look for the helpers and I was glad I could help people even if I was the last one to get out from my floor, I couldn't have lived myself if I hadn't done everything I could and I did. I don't know maybe it was God's will. It's not like I knew I would make it out but after a loud boom I thought I sort of had a feeling and all I can do is keep on walking. And then I finally sit on the ground as the smoke came in more and more.

Present

JEN

Sometimes I feel robbed you know. I was six when my mom died. Old enough to remember bits and pieces but too young to see it all in color and old enough to feel the guilt for forgetting. I had two moms you know. Mama Kathy and Angela the one who cuddled me and waited up all night after prom and heard all about my first crush. I used to say mommy went to heaven, but mama Angela is here now. As hard as it was on me wondering and crying myself to sleep, I remember dad crying himself to sleep many a night. It was harder on him. I'm glad he found her. He made it easier for her and all of us really. No, I can't imagine life without Angela, and Jimmy Jr and dly my Irish twin.

Sitting there though watching my dad die , I realized at one point that I was going to be an orphan .I have no Mom . No of course I had Angela but still it's a surreal feeling to realize that you would have been alone .I can count on her like a mom she's always there for me and I know she always will be and I feel so lucky. She's always been there and I know she always will .I cry just thinking about her. Some people say oh your stepmom and I say no she's more than that she's my mom she's my mother and it's true , she's everything I can wish for there's no regrets no wishing I had more . I'm really glad that my dad found her,that they found each other and there's a bonus I feel so happy and daddy always told me I had that Mommy and I have mommy Angela so I grew up knowing I had two mommies I thought everyone did .

Like I said I remembered mom in bits and pieces. One of my earliest memories is when I was five and Dad came in, in his firefighter uniform and sits by the table watching Mom paint my nails and I show them to Daddy and I say isn't it pretty and he says yes your mother knows how to make things pretty. Mom smiled and dad was like so how's my girls she said fine and he went outside and she continued painting my nails telling me how pretty I looked. Sometimes I feel bad about remembering her. Angela is such a good mom she's the only mom I really know but I know she knew I had to hold on. She even let me have a picture of her up in the living room ,Angela was a great mom I had two mommies one in heaven and one taking care of me right here on Earth. I guess I was blessed that way but still sometimes what I wouldn't have given to have just one more day.

ANGELA

There is no rewind. Yeah I know there is no rewind button but sometimes when I catch a glimpse of a flicker and see Jimmy's Junior's eyes and he laughs, I swear it's Jimmy senior and I smile it's not disloyal I know I would have ended up with him forever, we were that couple but it really isn't just loyal as much as I love him. I do love Tim too he's my angel he saved my life he made everything better but Jimmy he was my soulmate.

I can never forget, I often remember all the times that Dylan and Jimmy senior played football in the yard.I know Dylan did not like football but he really did at the time and maybe he just stopped liking it cuz it reminded him too much of his dad. I know he always says to me ,I hate football and dad would have hated it that I didn't like football but you know what I don't think that's true I think it's what they call a defense mechanism that's what I learned in counseling. Anyway I think Dylan hated football because it remind him of something that he could never get back not that he isn't a great writer and everything he's won all kinds of awards and the world might be less of author I mean maybe he would have still wrote anyway maybe that was his destiny but at least he would have had Jimmy his dad but no matter what I'll never forget the way Dylan ran out the door as soon as Dad came home and Jimmy would wink and smile at me and kiss me. I told him dinners in a half an hour. Dylan lived for those nights that Dad would come back, and he would get to play until dark and toss the football around. After his dad died, he would just wear the helmet for weeks and then he tossed it never looking back ,but anyway I remember always saying dinner soon and them saying the same thing I'm not hungry go to practice right Dad and Jimmy would smile and say hey everyone's got to eat dinner baby and then listen to your mom. I'll never forget the last practice it was just before 9/11 unbelievably hot I guess global warming and all they say but he is playing and he's playing with them and getting to do the the right pass and training them for peewee football. I know he had high hopes that dly would be a mini player and play football in college and he was good, but I guess we'll never know if he would have played or not but yeah that last day he played until dark, and I think dinner did get cold, I can still them and me saying come in. And smiling when Jim said ah five more minutes and Dly begged me too. Come in mom he said. We did eat just an hour later.

I know Dylan remembers all those memories. I know he does I think he finally admits it now, I was talking about a game on Saturday all through dinner. He was talking about the game the game that never happened cuz 9/11 and I couldn't take him. Because I had the baby , but nine months before that I told him I was pregnant at a game where I swear, I saw Jen as a little cheerleader and her cute little Junior cheerleader outfit with Kathy cheering her on and Tim smiling at her and that's where I told him I was pregnant this was 9 months before 9/11 even happened. I'm sorry I said to my daughter I'm all over the place. My daughter who is filming me because she is an amazing photographer and documentary filmmaker just smiles and says it's okay as I cry bucket of tears. As I look through the photo albums at Tim and I think why... why. Tim did save my life he really. He saved everybody's life. He was that kind of guy, and he would hate for me to say it but it's true God bless him he's an America hero. I'll tell you this though I didn't care that he was a hero or that what he did to help people in the building on 9/11. When I think about it later on I just wish that he was there with me and sometimes I think about it and I wish and I imagine that he was with me. That makes things a little better.

TIM

Everyone calls me a hero. I don't know. I don't know if I really am or not, but I know it's always saving lives that's what I love to do. That morning was the worst one and I always remember running down the street fast looking for someone to save trying to make it to the 100th floor where Kathy was but someone keeps distracting as I said before. I am sad I never made it. I wonder if I had what would have happened. People are coming downstairs screaming but I keep running upstairs I tell people where to go and I run more and more. That day there was no short of people to save of course. I know I mentioned this before but I think I heard a man scream for help but the moment passes me and I have to grab someone who fell and rushed them down and I tell someone to get to the 100th floor pronto to save him but I guess it was too late but after I take the lady down I run back up and I make it to the 40th and then I run back down and run up . I think before the towers fell, I had run up and down the stairs at least 10 times. That 10th time I heard a loud bang and I barely made it out. I never made it to the 100th floor. I just never did they call me hero, but I wish I could have saved everybody that day. The real heroes are the ones that never made it out. Those are the heroes.

Past

ANGELA

I screamed as I see someone fall from the building, I wondered was it him? Was it my Jimmy?

It couldn't be I whispered because Jimmy was coming home , Jimmy was going to be around to see our son walk and talk and I start to push. I have a contraction and I push harder I said I think of all the things that Jimmy will see, Graduation and marriage, grandkids and going all together. I see him fall again and I close my eyes. And open my eyes and see my Jimmy in front of me.

JIMMY SR

Push baby push. I tell my wife to push and I take her hand. She squeezes hard, almost too hard. Ouch I say . And she glares at me. She says that's pain try pushing something the size of a watermelon out of well you know... I move my hand back and tell her to push you're almost done. I say calmly. She frowns again how do you know are you psychic but she sighs. And she breathes. So I let her squeeze my hands until they're red and I can't bare it but I don't say anything. The doctor comes in and pushes me aside and I go to the bottom of the bed. I watched for the baby to come out and she keeps pushing and screaming and I keep telling her to breathe. Finally the baby comes out it's a boy I say it's a boy and I touch him and I smile. And I whisper your daddy's little boy and I know he smiles. It's impossible for there to be a smiling baby but I know he smiles and he knows me already. You are going to be the most amazing football player ever. I love you so much and your mommy loves you so much and your little brother loves you wait until you meet him and I call in my boy Dylan and he smiled and his brother and kisses him and I kiss him and I hand the baby to his mom my beautiful wife and we all hug. In that moment it is perfect just for a moment. I'm not just for a moment but forever it'll be a lot more perfect moments like this this is just the beginning I take a picture with the camera I'm holding of mommy and baby together and my wife squeezes my hand. She smiles at me and I kiss her on the cheek.

Angela

I'm sitting in my bed giving birth to my son and I feel my my husband kissed me on the cheek and I smile and I open my eyes and the doctor tells me to push ,my husband's not there. But in my mind he is. I look up and I see the TV and in between my contractions I go to the screen and say get up get up he doesn't.

The nurses smile at me, I'm trying to get them to turn off the TV and hand me my baby my newborn baby that needs me. He always needed me Jimmy always needed me I always held him close. I hold my held my baby closer than I did doing because he was all that I had left even though he's a big soccer player now when he was 10, he was a bookish and wasn't until Tim, that I could let him just a little to go on field trips. But that day I was scared well I wasn't scared really I was in denial. Close my eyes again I just imagine my husband was with me. I could feel him, feel his presence and all that made me smile because I know whatever he was doing he was there. I knew I would see him again. I just knew it. And I just pushed and I kept pushing until my baby came out and I felt Jim smiling at me and I didn't know anything at that moment but I did know one thing he was hovering over me and it wasn't until later on that I knew he was my guardian angel, protecting me. That was the beginning he was always there for me and he always was always was.

Present

Angela

It wasn't until Tim came in the picture and helped guide me, that I realized how much he needed a dad to let him be who he wanted to be. Not that a mom can't do that but but I knew a boy always needs a dad . We had his dad Jimmy senior he was always watching over him and be his guardian angel and he had his dad Tim here on Earth guiding him for all the things Jimmy couldn't do. I knew his name was going to be Jimmy and I had him I guess you can call it intuition. Whatever it was it felt good to wrap them in my arms and just hold them and I knew he was going to do big things. As he grew up he did a lot of amazing things.

Jimmy Jr , he got into sports never football though. He just fell into soccer, and he was good. I know Jimmy would have been proud he would have been out there learning how to play soccer.

He didn't know a thing about it, but he would have, he would have been out there until dark I told Jimmy Junior that often enough and he'll just look at me, but I say it's true. And I wrap around an arm around Jimmy protectively and I asked Dylan to have you thought about college and Jimmy just smirks said that guy he didn't even pick up a book and that was true he never did. I owe debt to Timmy he turned the whole family around I can't say it enough how much he changed. I was a mess. I was a hot mess . For instance I dropped off the kids on the first day of school. And I turned and I know Jimmy senior was there and I said to him where is Time gone and he looks at me and he smiles they're so big and I tell him I know and we hug and kiss and he tells me how proud they are he is of them and I turn and I look and he's gone . He's gone all I see is a news reporter with the camera saying today begins a new chapter for the kids and it's true it was Jimmy's first day of school. Where has Time gone indeed. Later that day later that week that month that year I don't know I lost so much time drinking I wouldn't even let him in. I was in therapy, but I couldn't let it go. I promised myself I wasn't going to forget. Every year on 9/11 I cried and cried no matter how I tried I couldn't let it go. How could I though really?

I just drank more and more until the kids came home one day. and Jimmy wanted to go on a thing, on a field trip and I said no, and he said come on it's the same one that Dylan went on and I said I don't care you know anything can happen and I wouldn't let him go and Dylan said come on Mom it's the same one I went to. But I say no it's too much you know anything can happen and I slam the door shut and that's that, but I do let him go. I feel bad.

I drop them off and let him go thanks to Dylan but that was my low point and I remember as Dylan and Jimmy drove off I remember crying oh Jim. And I remember screaming and I remember seeing Dylan looking scared and then Tim looks, and he offers to take Dylan and I watch the bus go and I cry, and I cry, and I cry, and I hug the thin air. Tim drives off with Jen and Tim looks at me through the rear-view mirror as if he's scared. I tried to straighten up, but I don't think he buys it. The first of many times did he rescue me. And that was the worst day of my life. After that I started going to meetings that they held for 9/11 and that's where I got closer to Tim, we both went, and the kids went, and drew pictures and we all got help here and we all got closer. It helped the kids to come there, and it helped me too. Helped me get sober and I started to miss Jim a little bit less. It wasn't just because I was getting to know Tim. Also, because the kids were growing and so was I. We were healing. We are finally able to move on, a little. I watched him hug Jennifer and I saw what a great dad he was and smiled at Jennifer. As Dylan and her became fast and furious friends. They've always been there for each other always. They've always been their lifelines. At one point I thought they were going to get married but I jump ahead. At eight years old they follow each other at twelve years old they follow each other, and they're joined at the hip. I think it was their first crush, but they needed it and it was great we got to do everything together. I didn't want Dylan to forget but the Red Cross lady assured me that kids needed to be healing and it was, and they did, and they needed to heal. All the sudden Jen started to cry and Tim rushes over. This happens sometimes he says to me. Daddy she cries you came. I always will always be here for you, Tim says. And he hugs her, and I see what a great dad he is how beautiful he is for his kid. I smile the first real smile I've had forever. The Red Cross lady sees it and smiles as if she saying it's okay for you too you can smile, and Tim tells Jen he'll keep every promise he ever makes and he did he always did every promise. Tim seemed to remember his Kathy because of his daughter Jen. I was having issues of my own it seems like every chance I got I remembered Jimmy. Mostly because of Dylan as I said Dylan was into football when he was young. And him and his dad would play all the time he played so much. I don't think there was one night that I didn't see them playing in the yard. I can still see him know they would play until dark I can just look out into the yard and see him playing smiling to me. Telling Dylan catch it buddy. Daddy helps me with that, a young Dylan says . I shake my head looks up and sees an empty yard and gets a little Misty eye and closes their eyes again and sees Jimmy by her side. He needs this you know. I shake my head. Tim just stares at Angela and takes one hand of his and says come on do it babe do it for me, please you know how much the game meant to me I nod and say okay and when I look up again, he's gone and I'm crying but I know what to do. It's been about a year and a half. I tell doing he can play again if he wants. The little boy that fell asleep in his helmet all the time was ecstatic when I took him to the field. I saw the coach right off and he smiled and welcome Dylan to the field. I saw him high five of his friends and I knew this was the right decision. I knew this was the best thing and the red cross helped me get there. I pick up Jimmy Jr and hold them tight. Your daddy loved football you know and then I started crying because I realize there's not going to be anyone to teach him to play it breaks my heart. Your daddy would have been great to teach you how to play. I say as I kiss him on the cheek. I look up and I see Jimmy Sr going down at me and smiling at Jimmy junior he'll be a natural you know. Have you seen that little guy run, I think he's going to be a running back don't you and I looked up at Jimmy and in that moment, Jimmy says yep, all natural? I look up the field and watch the kids playing and out of the corner of my eye I see Jimmy senior applauding and jumping up and down. I was doing the right thing. I looked up right then and I saw Tim staring and I nod. And Tim edges closer to me and sits next to me. Kathy would be so proud. I totally understand. We were both doing this for our spouses our dead spouses. I woke up and I see Jennifer and I smile she looked like an angel and tell Tim just as much. Tim Smiles and nods. I know right away. But whenever things get tough I always go to what if and I imagine that parallel life. It gives me comfort, it really does. To know Jimmy's with me no matter what and that he's watching and I know he does wish that he could do things different. Knew he would do whatever he had to differently if he could anyone. In Another reality he is with us and I have him and my babies and we're happily married for 20 years, well about 30 years really .

JIMMY SR

I wish I had gone with my wife. I rushed to work. Like I said and I got to my floor about a half hour before that's all I remember. I was on the 90th floor when the worst when the first world trade center plan hit being an unofficial firefighter I was a volunteer I took it upon myself to organize everybody. I did call my wife first and tell her I love her in case I didn't get out and from there I got everyone safe walking down the stairs we found the exit and kept moving I finally made it to the stairs and they kept walking and we came upon the first exit and I heard some pounding and I open the door and people came bearing out and I went in and they were like no don't go and I said I have to so I went to the floor and I got a couple people out of the office space and then every floor where they had an emergency exit and I made sure people kept walking. I think I got out a lot of people that wouldn't have gotten out. That was my job I feel like that was my job to help save people.I did what I had to do and if it wasn't for me hundreds of people would no have got out . I just remember talking to everyone and guiding them calmly to the stairs and told him where to go that was it. I was the volunteer fire warden from my floor. I guess I was chosen because I was the only one who had fire experience. I mean I did train at the academy my wife knew I was a volunteer fire Warden too .Yeah I took my job very seriously. I kept thinking in the back of my head I have to make it down I have to make it down. I have to make it to my wife but then I heard another little voice saying you got to help these people I couldn't live with myself and I know if I actually just walked down I would have been down a lot quicker and I would make it . I would have made it but I didn't so I took the time to really help all my people and all along I was just praying to my sons and my wife and I was praying to God while I was putting a smile on my face to the people still left you couldn't make them get out but most of them came out but gosh people could be fighting but not today. They want to hurry to go. I was too but I didn't care. And when I heard another explosion I went towards the last exit and I found a phone and called my wife I told her I loved her and I love the kids. I told her that I'll always be there for her and if she ever needed anything just look up.I didn't have time to think about where she was but I had a feeling that she was in labor and that she was having my child that I would never get to meet but I told her take care of my boys and teach him how to play football and I laughed. You wouldn't think one could laugh at a moment like that but that's all you had so yes I laughed but I knew my wife would get it because she knew me she knew that I was there for her but she knew what I was trying to say, I knew the call would be hard to get but I was glad I left it. Then the phone got disconnected and that was it and the smoke is getting to me and I coughed and I prayed and that was it and then I ran fell to the ground. Past

Angela

Yeah my husband called me . He called me. Through all the loud noise and ruckus I heard his voice and I kept that tape for so long.

He told me that he was helping people escape and then he was on the way down and their is another explosion and that he's going to be okay and just talk to the boys for me. He knew he was having a boy and there's a loud boom and that was it. I could hear his voice saying I'm going to make it I'll see you and that was it. I could tell he was scared. That last call when him saying goodbye I just kept crying and saying no .I want to say come down .I got it a couple days later as I had a newborn in my arms after the hospital and cried into my son's face and I nursed him. And I just listened. I didn't say anything but I wanted to say I hate you for not surviving but I couldn't say that because it wasn't the truth and for days all I could do is cry and I couldn't say anything. I guess I had survivors guilt. and I was depressed, I guess I had post pardon depression. Who wouldn't right. Makes sense but I would just hug my baby tighter and whisper. I know that I was in a bad place now and I knew that my mom was there for me. She helped a lot and that was the only thing that saved me because everywhere I looked I saw his face. Every time the boy opened his mouth , every time he cried. I tried to tell my mother this and I don't think she completely understood only knew my grief but still. I told him that he looked just like his dad I said, you just like him and even a little part of me wondered if he came back that quick. I don't know if that's possible but if it was, I'd like to think that had a small part of him. I'm just looking at Jimmy Jr and I already knew he was a lot like his dad .Every little sound he made and every facial gesture. I guess that's why I cried even harder. I just wondered if he had survived, I mean I know he was passed and that was sad but I clung on to that hope for days that hope that maybe he got out somewhere safe and then I would hear from him very soon . Yeah I'm very proud of Jimmy how can I not be. He was the hero he was the ultimate hero doing what he had to do and every 9/11, I pray for him even though I'm remarried now .One can't help but feel sad. You know. I wish I knew what else to say but I don't it's hard to say thank you. But I'm saying thank you thank you to everybody and that day to everyone who helped him thank you. He helped other people too and he helped people and it all comes full circle. Knowing that he was a fireman and that he was a helper yeah sure I wish he would have come home but you know what I rather that he did not come home and that he helped people and I put all those tapes somewhere safe so the kids could listen to him whenever they wanted and so I could listen to them and believe me I did .I almost bled the tape I listened to it so much and every time I listen to it I became prouder of him. I don't know how I could ever love anyone else again and that's what I thought everyday and that's why I couldn't be anything more with Tim. Tim did help pull me out of my despair. If it wasn't for him I'm just been stuck. I'm glad they didn't give up on me. I loved him but I lived Jim Jr too . I could never choosen but I do know this sometimes you do have more than one soulmate in the lifetime .All I can say is we got this but I tell my kids everyday especially now we got this as Jimmy would have wanted me to say. I knew Jimmy would have liked him and I mean they did have a lot in common they had the whole fire fighting thing and so that helped me go for Tim. I mean I knew that Jimmy would have wanted me to be happy but still I needed that sign and I got it. Tim was always there for me he was my savior. I couldn't be any more happier truly I couldn't and I do look up to the sky every night and I feel like I hear him laughing or just giving me a one too and saying really babe or why are you doing that with the kids that's worried our nightly conversations for the longest time. And then there's Tim.

TIM

I fell in love with her right away. Our circumstances were different. She loved him and I was getting a divorce. Not many people knew that. How could I tell them? It seems so cold. But it's true. When she died there was no love lost, but I pretended there was, who wouldn't, right? Though I got to be more a father. If Kathy had lived, I know that I would have seen less of my little girl. After, family became more important. Angela and I bonded, and our love grew slowly through the pain. Slowly we grew and became a family. I was there for Jimmy Jrs first words, taught him to ride his bike and healed his broken heart when his crush didn't like him back. I did what any dad would do. Slowly she, dyl, Jimmy jr and Jen all became one. No, we never forgot, how could we but through the pain we formed an unbreakable bond. We still deal with the pain and the memories, but it helps to have true love. I do Wonder though in a different reality what would have happened with me and Kathy. It's like my daughter says if she had played sick

Kathy who have wanted to stay home that day. I close my eyes and try to imagine and I open them.

I touch my daughter as we hear a horn honk and I tell my daughter to go her mom's waiting. I look out the window and I wave and Kathy waves. I have my daughter and say see you Monday. My daughter runs out the door then she comes back and kisses me. Runs back out to her mom and then drives away. I opened my eyes and rub them and look around and there's nothing. But I imagine what would have happened. I throw myself in the work and helping others and try to not think about what ifs , just what is. But I know somewhere there's always a different reality. I don't know anything at the time I just know I have to do my job. That's what I do and I just focus on right now.

KATHY

Finally the smoke was hitting so bad and there's nothing to do I lay there on the ground and I tried not to cry. There was a phone and I picked up the phone . I kept thinking because I knew Tim was in the building somewhere where is he who's coming soon they'll send helicopters. All I knew is there was a fire I didn't know anything else and I heard a loud explosion. I picked up the phone and I called home and told him take care of her girl and yes I told him I loved him because regardless of anything I know I did and I knew he loved me. And then I hung up the phone and I cried just a tiny bit. Can I pick myself up and I made myself be strong and said I got this and I spent the rest of time just praying. There's only one person to the other side of me we were both trapped we couldn't see each other but I could hear her and I told her it would be okay and we both just prayed. Here I'm talking to her family and then nothing and then darkness. Present

JIMMY JR

So, I had no regrets of course. I just had pain watching my dad get weaker and weaker and weaker . Who would my kids call grandfather. Now I can feel how Dylan felt. it does feel odd though I scream how could 9/11 take this away from me again. I Wanted to go to

Afghanistan and kill everybody. To kill all the bad guys for taking my father away almost 20 years later that's a sad part. Is later we're still paying the Piper,so to speak nothing good my generation. We didn't get to graduate high school cuz of covid and we lost so much of our innocence during 9/11, we always will and lose everything, but we learn to live with it and just get through it it's all you can do. I learned from my mom. Dad said she was a survivor, and she would have done anything to help anybody, but I also know that's me, but I also know that I'm surviving I couldn't look fear in the face, and I say whatever and bullying myself through I got it not just because my mom because of the world I inherited.

DYLAN

Fuck those bastards. I wish I was the one to give it to Osama bin linden. I volunteered for the marine's special forces because I remember that morning, but I didn't get the role. I'm just glad someone got him finally! I was six when my life changed forever. My dad was taken. I know he was a hero. He loved football, that was his game. We played every Sunday and watched it on TV every Monday till mom made us turn it off. I think that's what I missed the most, no more football after that morning. I wonder what I would be if Daddy Jimmy hadn't died. My real dad, we called him, my mom encouraged, so we would have no guilt and papa Tim the one who cuddled me and waited up all night after prom, didn't have that same passion for football. I think mom liked that though. I still played in high school though but without that passion. My passion was getting the bad guys. I used to say daddy went to heaven, but papa Tim is here now, but I still got to go get the bad guys for daddy Jimmy. As hard as it was on me wondering and crying myself to sleep, I remember it was harder on mama. And I'm glad she found Tim. He made it easier all of us. I can't imagine life any different, but I want all those who killed daddy Jimmy friggen dead. That's what I always think. When I was in the military I always felt my dad . I even saw him sometimes . When I was in the foxhole a couple times fatigue does all heck I looked around and I knew I was having conversations with him. No one else is around in the dark and the quiet in the desert he was my guardian angel. Told me how to protect myself, told me how to live. Told me to make a left or righ,t to not light a cigarette etc etc. Crazy or not I listen to every word because I knew. No the last thing Angela needed was to lose me. That would have devastated her. He told me no I am not god but he did his best to watch over him and gave me signs. Dad I'm listening I said. Daddy I know you're here and he said I know you are listening to me. Because the proof is that your alive. I know it wasn't your time to go he said . He was not going to let me go. Did everything in my power to protect me .Daddy said to me , I know you are listening because I saw you every now and then look around like you felt me. I couldn't have been prouder of you my boy. So I always watched out for my dad because he I knew he would be around whenever I needed him real or imagined he was like my God.

I will never forget that day the day twenty years ago. I don't know what I'd be if my dad had lived. My dad was a big football coach he loved football. Me I wasn't so good, I tried maybe I tried harder because he was gone, and he died he was in the towers that day. But you know what if he had lived, I probably wouldn't have played football anyway. I wasn't good but I would have tried and then I would have hated him, and we would have spent five years just hating each other as it is I became a writer. I was a little too sensitive to play football instead I write novels. I write novels. Tim did not encourage me to play football while he was a rough and tumble kind of guy but still I don't know maybe it's cuz he wasn't a blood father, but he was the only dad I knew. But we didn't clash he didn't try too hard so I could become the writer I was destined to be that day. As a writer I often change the reality and imagine what the conversation would have been like with my dad.

JIMMY SR

Come on Dylan try harder I tell my boy . You want to play football, you want to make the team don't you. We only have a half hour more to practice you can do this kiddo.

Dyl runs into the house and I hear him crying. There he catches me telling Angela that I know I pushed him too hard and then I'll apologize tomorrow. I tell Angela I hope he doesn't hate me she smiles and says you're here , he could never hate you. I'm not so sure but I smile at her and I see Dylan around the corner and I wink at him and I hug him and like a boy he cries and runs but then comes back and tells me he's sorry let's try one more time Dad I'll try harder for you.

DYLAN

Bye daddy I whisper . I wave goodbye as he disappears.

I was only seven that day and there was no what ifs dad went to work at 7:00 , I didn't even get to say goodbye to him. Mom dropped me off at school she was pregnant with Jim Junior and was about to pop boy was she big, but when we didn't know if she was going to pop that day and of course what we didn't know is that Dad would never see Jimmy. I am glad that I knew dad. But you know what he would have liked Jimmy Jr I mean of course he would have loved him, but Jimmy Jr is an athlete through and through. They would have bonded.

Sometimes I regret that but I'm glad I had Tim because even though he's a bit rough and tumble guy and firefighter he has a soulfulness to him that I got to love that encouraged me to write that no one else understood but Dad also would have liked it Jimmy Jr more because he played soccer. It was not his choice as I mentioned but anyway, I had a flash back to day one D-Day as we call it and of course I didn't know Jennifer she was just a girl and it's 7:00. I did not like girls, but I just remember seeing some girl Jennifer doing cartwheels. I knew of her, but I didn't know her but that morning I digress yet again that morning Mom dropped me off as I said she was about to pop but Mom dropped me off. and I remember the teachers pulling in the little TV car you know so we can watch TV the 9/11. They pulled it in, and I remember the teachers crying and the principal coming on and saying everyone please go to the gym something very bad has happened and your parents will come and get you of course dad didn't he was trapped. Mom later I would find out was having Jimmy her water broke an hour after but as the seven year-old I waited and waited and even Jen the girl doing cartwheels was gone. I waited in the gym until more people were gone and then the cafeteria where there was twenty of us and then ten and then finally the principal took me into his office and said when you come in here and read and so I read. I pulled out my book and I read was a good escape and finally the principal looked at his watch and said let's go outside and so we did. I sat on the steps, and he squeezed my hand. I don't know if he knew but I liked to think he did. I wish I was older, and I would have asked but I think he knew but he was there to protect me, nonetheless.

I'm with Tim now. I'm watching him get weaker and weaker.

Very hard but as I look at him all the memories flashed to my mind everything, he did for me, and I smiled him, and he squeezes my hand. And I know he's remembering too. Can tell from that far off look on his face.

Even though I was a little kid I still ,I still imagined how things could be different. I knew things are wrong. I had a feeling I would never see my daddy again. It was just because I was little and I had that connection with the other world or maybe it's because he visited me but I cried and I close my eyes and I saw my daddy. My dad's running to me and I smile and we hug.

JIMMY SR

I see my son standing with the principal and I hold him. And I say let's go. Where we going dad and I say we're going to get your favorite steak and cheese sandwich. He smiles and says won't mommy be mad. I tell him no don't worry about it we got this and me and him take off , we play the music in my truck. We're just laughing. I always remember that night and I tell Dylan to remember that too. Tell Dylan it's an important day in history and never forget 9/11 and we're celebrating the fact that you have a new baby brother. And that tomorrow I'll take him to see his baby brother.

DYLAN

I opened my eyes and I look around and I'm still with them . The principal was looking at me with pity in my eyes.That's the way it should have happened. Dad should have taken me out for supper and we should have had a great night celebrating my baby brother and the next day yeah we should have went to see the baby. I guess that day really changed my life and there's no going back. I know that Mom knows that Jen knows that. No way you can reverse history. I only wish.

I only wish I had a time machine. Oh if things have been different I wouldn't have been troubled. Mom wouldn't be in trouble and dad would have been happy and Jimmy too.

Though as it was we went to all kinds of meetings and had all kinds of therapy. We had to do what we had to do to keep sane. But deep down I was just a boy who wants my dad. We just wanted things to be just a little bit different. I remember we went to a lot of meetings. The friends of the firehouse. Where I met Jen and Tim. Mom would take us and I would color and she would just hold the baby.

Mom always says Dad was meant to be a firefighter. He wasn't really a pencil pusher. Had he lived he would have quit and become a firefighter or volunteer or something. I know I said. I told Mom I knew and she would hug me. With that distant look in her face. And I would see my dad staring at me just watching us. And I would whisper to him telling him I loved him.Telling him to come home.People would watch me talk and they didn't say a peep but they just told me to get it out on paper and I would just smile because ,I knew what they didn't know. I knew that the Angels were with us all the time. Daddy I would say why where are you and he would tell me heaven baby. I stood before me watching me paint on the paper and he would tell me that looks good. I told him thank you and that I loved him said that again and again and he said that he loved me again and again. He told me he was glad that I was healing. To feel him watching over my shoulder and being proud of all the work I was doing and I knew that he knew how much I missed him. Was indeed my guardian angel. All that work I was doing to heal would pay off and help me become the artist I am today and I still know Daddy Jimmy's with me, no matter what people say and he was with me all along.

ANGELA

About a few weeks after Jimmy senior died, I started going to friends of the firehouse. Told this was a great place to go. Being that my Jimmy was a firefighter of sorts I found refuge with other firefighters' wives, and they all supported me and hugged me, and I ran from it, but I went to the the friends of New York firefighters' group because I could cook there and just be I spent all my spare time there.

I brought the new baby and everyone googled over him and I brought Dylan who love being around all the firefighters.He was a little too young to understand what was going on but still I knew he was sad and I knew he realized he just said over and over again when's Daddy coming home . So even though some level he knew Daddy was gone we had a ceremony, still couldn't comprehend and that was the hardest part I didn't know whether to tell him that he's gone daddy died and keep telling him that over and over again or just him let him grieve. I ended up telling him you know Daddy went to heaven he's with Grandma. He would not and then a few days later he'd say it again. Went on for days and weeks and months, it felt like years. By the time Dylan was older of course, by older I mean eight he pretty much knew daddy was gone. By then Tim was a part of our lives. I first met him at the friend of the fire house where people told me he lost his wife too in the towers. I don't think they knew each other but I felt like Tim was my guardian angel and that Jimmy gave them to me that we were destined to meet somehow. Because of this I didn't want to jinx it. I just stayed friends with him for so long it felt right not to take it to another level, I didn't want to risk losing the friendship you know. Like it wasn't right. Brotherhood and firefighters. It was like they knew each other, and they worked in the same squad, and I was being disloyal it's the way I saw it. The last we bonded, and we took care of each other. And over the years our kids became best friends too and of course Dylan and Jen dated but that was all later as it was, we just became a little unit within a unit. It was a cocoon and it felt safe.

TIM

One of the first times I remember really talking to her, to Angela is when I saw her crying in her car. Sure, I seen her before of course at the friends of the firefighters in New York and all the mental health things we did for ourselves and for the kids, but this was different. This is real and personal, and I realized that we need to be there for each other. I saw the kids looking flustered and I asked the kids what was wrong, and they said mom's having a breakdown again and so I went over to help her, and I smiled, and she looked at me shocked to see me, but she still smiled, and I knew I was doing something right. I asked her what's wrong. Angela just cries harder, and I tell her I'll take the kids to school and her not just she grabs us doing well harder. I tell the kids come on and Jennifer and Jimmy Jr are ready for preschool follows me. I asked where the preschool is, and we drop him off first and then I take the kids to school, and they jump out of the car all smiles and happy. I realize kids are like that do not like adults they don't hold stuff for long they may be in pain, but they bounce back quick. After I see the kids are ok , I drive around, and I go back and Angela's still there and I knock on her window, and she looks up at me and rolled down the window and motion to unlock the door and I get into the car. I just sit there and be silent for a minute and I finally ask her what's wrong and she looks at me and I smile. And she left it all out telling him about field trips and everything. I say I understand. It's true I do understand, and I tell her we must let go sometimes. That's true too . As much as I was getting divorced from Kathy. I still had to let go myself cuz she wasn't there to be a pain in the ass too. She wasn't there to make custody arrangements with and take the court and figure out who was going to have Jen none of that was happening and I hated her for it I hated the situation for that. So yeah, I understood I circumstances may have been different but still it's still added up to the same thing you know. Angela looked at me and said I just can't. Don't you miss her and I nodded and said yes, all the time when I look at Jen, I see Kathy 100% of the time. It's hard but you know the right thing. Can I do something I regret well sort of regret I lean in and kiss her Angela first leaned in and kisses me and then pulls away I can't I just can't, and I lean out and get out of the car. I'm sorry I don't know why I did that. Angela just stares at me says it's okay but it's not. I mean I wanted to kiss her but maybe I was breastfeeding. I don't know I just don't know. Nothing makes sense anymore, but I don't regret it. I tell Angela it's been ten years and she just looks at me like I'm crazy and says I know almost right I can't even believe it myself. It's like he's still here. I feel guilty .I can understand that but I can't at the same time. He's not with her, not with me all the time. That's when I realize their connection was deep. He'd always be there watching over for her .I smile at her I tell her I do and the funny thing is I do understand at that moment I really do. But I tell her he'd want you to be happy and she says I know but I'll know when it's time, I'm glad we're friends. I nod. Friends there's that word not a bad word just complicated. I didn't just want to be friends, but I knew I had to. I knew for her it seemed like yesterday and I told her so and she said yeah it seems like just like yesterday.

ANGELA

After the baby was born after Jimmy Jr was born, I went to a lot of rallies I went to Rally's and the subways putting up signs and of course Grand Central station where everyone went looking at all the pictures. I was overwhelmed and I was convinced at first, I was doing this to find him I was convinced I'd find Jimmy. I didn't of course but then I got into it I channeled my passion, and everyone loved Jimmy he represented hope and I got happier doing something. A stewardess, she was supposed to be on a flight on 9/11 looks up at me and says it could have been me you know and that's all she says, and I look up and I see the tears in her eyes . She just thanks everyone for letting her speak and that's when I know and that's when I know we have to let go and I started to cry. Someone wipes away the tears in my eyes. I was finding peace and I was looking for Jimmy. I didn't know it at the time, but I don't think I ever gave up hope not ever around that same time that's when I found Al-Anon. That's when I went to the meetings I was in the church, and everyone was holding hands saying the serenity prayer. It made me have peace I created inner happiness for me.The group was saying God grant me the serenity to accept the things I cannot change and change of things I can and the wisdom to know the difference. And look out and I see Tim that's the first time I saw him. He's always been there for every little thing. I don't know what I'm going to do without him. I know now Jimmy would approve I don't know why I waited so long. But I did. But I did. I remember seeing him at the meetings and he would be supportive of me and say I understand, and we would talk, and we got the kids together for playdates and in the background the song imagine by John Lennon is playing and we're swinging back and forth and finding peace. It's hard to find that peace but it's possible.

The stewardess is speaking when I look up and she's saying how she was supposed to be on that fight and then how she was grateful for God for letting her live and the look up at her and she has tears and she is grateful that she's alive and they look out and see the Statue of Liberty and I feel Serene and peaceful for a minute I realize that's all we have is peace and I try to find peace and I cry and I wipe away a tear but I smile through my tears. I go to the Grand Central station where people are leaving notes and I write a note to Jimmy telling him that Jimmy's Juniors getting better everyday and then he looks like him and he's going to have that athletic talent and then he'd be so proud .I also say please hurry home that we all missed him. I put the note on the on the floor at Grand Central station and I walk away I've done my piece and as I walk away and look at all the notes for all the people I do cry. But I cry not just for Jimmy but for all the people who lost someone, for all the people trying to be family, just trying to live. You know I knew it wasn't healthy, but I couldn't stop, I couldn't stop believing that he was coming home for the longest time. I still set a plate at the table for him, I still talk like he was just working on the business trip. I would go to the meeting and tell everyone that he's coming back that every time I heard a car stop or a lot of noise, I thought he was coming. Everyone feels my pain. I even called all the hospitals and I called him regularly. Every week I'd call a different place for 5 hours in one day. I called every hospital and the next day I would start again and again and again, and they all knew it was me. But I knew everyone else was doing it too. Now we wouldn't stop until we knew. I abandon everything now even the kids. I would shoo Dylan away and Jimmy and thank God for my mom. The kids got taken care of and fed sometimes it got so bad Tim, would come by from next door. I was always seeing Jimmy Sr. In the house in the field. I remember one time, I just finished making calls for the day and I was about to take everyone for pizza. I couldn't do it and I just looked and luckily my mom was there she was taking the kids and Jimmy senior was getting mad at me he said don't do it. Remember our model kids first and I just cried even harder I can't, but I wiped away the tears and I said okay kids go for pizza go with Grandma. Mommy will be okay and in that moment I know I was going to be okay. I was going to be okay, everything was going to be okay, somehow. I didn't know how but I think that was a real turning point. I just kept hearing our motto is kids first, kids first. And I look out the window and I don't see Jimmy Jr, but I see Tim coming in looking tired and dirty.

TIM

Everyday I would go out to the fields of New York . Not really the fields, it felt like the fields though, the pile as we call it. I go out digging in the in the smoke and it ruined my lungs that's why I'm dying but I go out there every freaking day just digging and digging looking for him I'm looking for her and maybe even just looking for a piece of mind and then I would come home to Jen and my mom those two things save me knowing I was doing what I was doing and my baby girl. I had to be strong for my baby girl.

The things I remember in the days to come in the weeks and as the weeks turned into months was how hard it was to find no survivors and just the body parts and buckets it was tough. But I did it was my job and I felt good to do something I don't know about everyone else, but I said silent prayers on the field for every part we found. I thought of the families and the person it belonged to and cried a little bit on the inside and said a word of thanks you had to. Everyone goes then you would know that this is probably the most haunted place especially in the months we spent digging in the building they were all there just watching us you can imagine... if you like oh that's my hand that's my ...you know... that's my that or just laughing. It's hard to think about anybody laughing, I'm sure I will someday but for then and for now I'm laughing a little but for then I just had to pray that the laughter would continue or that it would come back, and it has and for that I'm grateful. Every time I see my daughter and I hug her look into her eyes and see her mom and every time I play with her, she makes me smile.

I don't give her the Moon and back that's why it hurts so much now to be losing myself, but I try not to think about that and just think of the now. If I didn't want to get mad ...I didn't want to think about what could be held up on purpose or not. Jen asks me to play with him and grandma says no don't worry he'll play with you later and I know.

I just couldn't do it I was tired I'm working too hard I know it, I knew it. I knew I had to be there for her, but I knew I couldn't, if I didn't keep working in the yards every day, I was going to lose my mind, I had to go there. This is my way of healing or maybe... I Just knew I was getting something out of my system maybe. I knew I was keeping her alive and maybe I didn't. Didn't matter all that mattered is that I needed happiness. And I was finding it. I used to see Angela at the friends' firefighters fire house. everyday going to the meetings for grief and one day I got the courage to talk to her and I told her thanks for sharing she nodded, and I told her I understood, and we hugged each other, and I truly did feel like I was a part of something in that moment something deeper something real. It was nice to be a part of something where people understood you. Saying you keep going back and I did I keep going back and I finally healed, and I found peace of mind. Angela and I got closer, we went for coffee, we had food and enjoyed the company. I'm not going to say it was easy because it wasn't. She was struggling emotionally and financially. She told me once why can't he be still be alive I didn't know what to say to that, There's nothing I could say really I had to give her that hope but we got closer we bonded the months became the days became months the months became years and we just found our routine the kids grew older and I still had our routine I was fine but let go of her a long time ago if it hadn't been for her holding on to him, Jim, I would have done something sooner. I know it couldn't have been I had to say where I was at and stay in my lane it's not because I was afraid of losing her. I respected him too much. And then there was the kids I didn't want them to think it was replacing their dad, but I tried to be them there for them God knows they needed it. And of course, Jen needed a mom figure not that I could ever replace her, but I just knew I couldn't do this alone and what a better place when someone that understood the firehouse and that way of life. Or even so I knew it didn't feel right to jump in I knew she didn't want to jump in, so I just let it go slow that's why the first time I saw her outside of the firehouse, or such a big deal and I was able to get some wiggle room and start to go to her house and that's when things really part in the pun heated up. The times I came over to the house I would just sit there watching TV and sometimes we just watch late night TV and not say a peep and just eat and that was enough to really help each other I knew that's what she needed, and I needed too.

DYLAN

Night after night I would come down and Mom would just be watching David Letterman I would tell her mom turn it down and I would ask her if she needed any help with the bills she barely would say anything to me that she was drinking bottle and she just turned the TV on. Mom never even packed her lunches. I got us lunch money for the next day. When we left for school mom was drinking wine and day time TV and when we came back, she was watching soaps and drinking more wine. A friend Marge made dinner for us made sure we had clean laundry and she always asked about field trips unlike mom. I was there for Jimmy like no one else would have been I listened to him tell all about the museum of natural History and all the dinosaurs and that was hard for Mom, but it was hard for me too, but someone had to be there for Jimmy he didn't ask for all this mom was just numb eating her carrots, but I listened on and on. Jimmy and I go to bed before I go to bed I turn around and there's mom on the couch drinking more wine with the TV loud, but I see Marge and I know Marg just got this ,she winks at me when I smile. I hear her tell Mom that she looks like a zombie, and she needs to clean up her act and then she leaves, and I noticed the TV is off and I hear mom talking out loud I hear the name Jim I know she's not talking about my brother.

JIMMY SR

Baby it's going to be okay. You have to take care of the kids, you have to stop drinking baby. I'm getting scared. The promise we made to each other we said if anything happened to each other we take care of our kids and give them everything they needed. Angela just looked at me and stared and I got in her face and kissed her on the cheek like in our favorite movie Ghost. Is to say that was the most romantic movie. She would look up cuz she felt and on her cheek and she would smile and say I know. I know what I need to do and I said I know you do and I know you will.

ANGELA

That night after Marge leaves, I see Jimmy senior again. He asked me well let's say well what he yelled at me am I going to get off the couch and grab the bowl by his horns I look at Jimmy and look upstairs and back at Jimmy and he's gone. I hear a scream and run upstairs the kids are safe in bed and I took them in again and tell them good night it was supposed to be good night.

I quietly turn off the lights and wonder what happened but at least it got me off the couch that's all I have to say. The next morning I'm a little better I even managed to make breakfast and lunch for the kids no lunch money. Today I am taking them to school. Dylan looks at Jimmy Junior, Angela winks at him. Hey good old mom's raring to go and Dylan gets a smile and then Jimmy Jr smiles and we're all smiling Jimmy smiles as if to say you're back and I say yeah, I'm back. At dinner Dylan goes on to say and we had oatmeal for breakfast and everything. Marge looks at me tells the kids yummy. I'm going to a meeting I say . She nods and smiles. I get to the meeting and I'm happy I'm very happy and I see Tim and I sit next to him and he smiles and grabs my hand as he coughs and I look concerned and he says it's just allergies don't worry. I know it was a good meeting and after the meeting we go for lunch somewhere and have a great time we talk and chat and for the next few weeks we're together non-stop with the kids in the backyard and the baseball games and the football games but Tim is still coughing and I tell him you need to do something about that cough. He just laughs everyone has it don't worry about it. He looks apologetic and he says don't worry about it it's nice to have someone worry for once and he tells me his secret that he was getting divorced . I'm shocked as they seem like such a great couple and he tells me he never told anyone .I look at the kids and they look at Tim and surprise I just stand there and watch the kids play at Twilight and grab fireflies. Tim coughs and Angela looks at him and says okay.

TIM

The next day I find myself going to the doctor at Angela's instance even though I knew what they were going to say the doctor asked me if I smoke. And I say no but I have been working at the 9/11 spot with the ashes and the smoke the doctor knows. Yeah, it's going to be a mess, you know it's all over the news. He says you can soon I said I don't want to see no one I just want to find a survivor or the bodies. The doctor nods and just for the record I never smoked. The doctor writes that in his pad and later that day I find myself behind a news desk and their interviewing me about all the work I've been doing. I tell him it's no big deal they act like I'm a hero they say we have Tim Zambia with us talking about his sickness and we have a retired fireman and they are and they asked what I'm going to do and I say I'm urging the Congress to vote on this now we helped and now we need their help and then I cough right on the air if right on cue. That It will help us get something on it and we both laugh. I say we need our America's help. I'm watching the news at Angela's that night she says without a doubt they'll pass the bill I just say I hope so . I don't have anything. I noticed that glazed look on Angeles's face and I know she's seeing Jimmy sr. I'm used to it but darn if I wouldn't like a new house, I want to move too but I know that's not the best for Jennifer, and she feels the same about the boys but if we had our own place, we wouldn't have to see him, and I wouldn't feel guilty. It wasn't my fault and she just smiled at me and asked if I wanted a beer. All the papers piled up in the yard and in the kitchen and the dining room and I asked her if she needs any help, she says yes but I can't take it. I don't want to lose the house she says I don't tell her anything. I know. I don't want her to lose the house. I can tell she's stressed out and I am too just because she is.

ANGELA

I'm throwing papers around my bedroom and ask Jimmy sr what do you want from me. I can't keep the house and he tells me you need to for the boys, and I say no I can't , I don't want to. I just want to move and I say it's just this is our history how they remember me. How they remember you . He tells me it doesn't matter they'll always remember me no matter where you are. Do what's best for the kids do what's best for you he says as he stands over me watching me cook in the kitchen. I can't have them forget you , I tell him. Well you know what you left, and I correct myself I know you didn't leave but still I'm left with all this mess I can't afford it. I don't know what to do he looks at me and says we'll figure something out we will. Dylan comes in and says he needs new shoes and I say that's it the next day I'm signing up for classes at the college and putting it for sale sign out. I don't care how mad my ghost is I won't talk to him for days as he storms around salty like it's my fault and I know it's not his but still. I am a survivor. Ultimately I know he's proud of me though and that's what he wanted me to do maybe I'm making it all up that he was sad and mad at me cuz I didn't want to deal with the reality. I moved on to college, got a degree and was even selling the house. Tim came to visit on the campus, and we had lunch and we laughed and giggled like school kids even though we weren't. And through it all I still saw Jimmy watching me and him me and Tim but I knew he was happy at the same time as sad as he was as sad as I was. I knew he wanted the best.

TIM

I would have lunch with her in the cafeteria some days on my lunch break and I even asked her if she wanted to move in with me, she said no but I couldn't live in someone else's house, and I told her I would sell there's no memory loss for me, so I sold it and then we told the kids they were okay about it they were happy. I know we'd make it. Sure, we were just sort of friends and dipping your toes in really like Harry met Sally my favorite movie hers too and I smiled I know we got this no matter what we were going to be good we were survivors we are survivors.

When I finally met Jimmy Jr, I realized I would have to step it up. I never had a son, but he was the closest thing I gave that boy in my heart and soul. I love Dylan too they are both my heart no more than

Jen but there's something about a boy it feels like you can train them you get a little part of yourself. There's nothing I could do for Angela there's nothing I couldn't do for her. And again, her boys, especially Jimmy Jr only because I got to be there from the beginning. Said I love Dylan, but he held back and that's not bad I expected it and it's not that I didn't encourage Jimmy to think about his dad and as we called him daddy Jimmy. Encouraged him too and he knew what I was.

I love him and I love Dylan too but still, there was a special bond with Jimmy Jr. I sit back now, and I cry. I sit back being sick and think back to those days and what I could have done different in hindsight. Would I do everything different but in reality... I did everything I could we were all suffering. In fact, I remember this one time on 9/11 Angela drove out to the New York and just sat there on the bench and saw all the names and I knew she was crying. I knew she was going to have a hard day and that was the day that Jimmy Junior had to get in trouble. I mean who is to blame them. It was 9/11 and his birthday when he had so many lame birthdays full of pain. I got the call and he was ten years old. I was the emergency contact by then and I was sad but I showed up with balloons and cake as he was just swinging and I let him just eat the cake and I let him cry and I told him next year we have a giant party and he smile as he popped the balloon one after another and stuffed the cake in his face and giggled the way only a 10 year old can giggle. He thanked me and I smiled. Someone told me there's a great kid you have there, and I said he's... and then I didn't say anything. I just smiled and thanked him. I suppose we did look like a father and son . We may not have looked alike not exactly, but we had that look I guess, and I knew he know that I would do anything for him. We just got in the car and drove I asked him if he alyas ready to bust the joint, he said yeah, and I signed the papers at school, and we were off. We just drove to the city and before we knew it, we were in front of the world trade center, and I saw Angela and Jimmy ran to her and she smiled they were both depressed and hugged. Tomorrow it would be busy but today was just a little bit of letting go. She saw the cake when we got back to the car, and she smiled at me and mouthed thank you and that was the last year she forgot a birthday .She promised him he she wouldn't, and she didn't.

Sitting here tonight I realize I've been around for every milestone of Jimmy. I'm specifically thinking of when he first came home from the hospital.

Next door neighbors let me know when she came back, I knocked on the door to see if she needed anything a little bit of food and I gave it to her and she's nursing the baby and I got to hold him right away. It was the nicest feeling he smiled up at me with his big eyes. I really say babies can't smile but he did. And I fell in love in that moment. As I was holding it. Angela came up to me and held me and asked me if you think he's still alive and I stared at her, and she said Jimmy senior I didn't know what to say. I just stared back I'm finally I blurted out no it was wrong timing. Dylan came down and saw me and he started to cry, and Angela cried then it's a nightmare I said but it's been a few months now he could come back. And she asked me how I was doing because of Kathy, and I told me, and Jen are fine we're holding up you know every day is getting better and better and she got all opinions and I wish I could say the same and she just cradled the baby to her. I looked at the ground and I said I think he jumped... she cries harder. I looked at the ground I mean I don't know I said I mean it's a possibility, but he did help people. She backed away from me she tells me to get out. I run to the door and then turned back. I just wanted you to know I thought you should know the truth. I didn't want too there. Angela cried harder why would he she cried she cried, and I told her I don't know to save himself he panicked. Maybe, I don't know, I don't know what you would do in that situation. Angela threw herself in in my arms and says oh Jim and I were supposed to be together and watch our kids grow up we were the couple everyone wanted to be. I tried to appease her and say I know, and some nutcase had to ruin it, but we must be we have to fight for those who can't for those that died. I look back at Angela and she's crying. The baby's crying and she just goes to nurse the baby and I run out of the house not knowing what to say. Last I saw them she was rocking Jimmy Jr , singing to him.

ANGELA

I don't know what to think when Tim told me the truth. I was mad, I was sad, I was confused, and I had a new baby ...I just wanted to believe he got confused. Maybe he had amnesia maybe Jim just had amnesia and that was it. I'm sorry I just chased him out. I couldn't hear it, but Jim Junior was my strength I would walk him to sleep every night hush little baby don't say a word don't you cry mama's going to buy you a diamond ring Papa's going to buy you a looking horse. I sang that song every night that was our song. I would nurse and I would sing, and I finally realized what I was saying, and I realized Papa's not going to buy you anything after months I just threw away the song, I didn't want to give him false hopes you know. Why stop singing the song you know I know people think I'm crazy, but I know Jimmy seniors with me I always feels his presence. and always see him and would tell me that he was always going to be there for me, and Jimmy Junior and Dylan and it made me feel good. Made me feel happy to know that I was being taken care of. And we sit there for months in that same routine I fell asleep to Jimmy senior and then Jimmy Jr would wake me up crying for nursing and I'd wake up at dawn and then we go back to sleep for a little bit and that would be time to get Dylan ready for school and then I go to sleep again and that's the way our life was simple easy breathing no stress but I guess I let it go on too long it came a crutch. Tim was going through his own stuff. I know I shouldn't have taken out on it out on him, but I couldn't help it. But gradually I let him in I'm out we did everything together we had barbecues and that's what we were.

In the summer and caught fireflies and he was there for Jimmy's first step and even when Jimmy needed a new big boy bed which I was surprised about Tim was the first one I told. He really supported me, we became best of friends. But with all that there was still Jimmy senior he was still there watching. Then there was Tim. He tried to take care of things. I didn't know it was all the the fun I needed. It really was my saving Grace as much as Tim was there for every first Jimmy was too and I couldn't I couldn't let that go when Jimmy was walking, Jimmy senior was there and say I'm so proud of him he's a big boy now your daddy's little big boy and I was glad for that without that I don't know what I would have done .I know I sound like a broken record but it's true and he said just like me you'll always make the right decision .Won't you .I swear Jimmy Jr smiled they looked right in his direction too and kids can see angels and that's what he was seeing his guardian angel but I said to him right decision. You may have made a thousand right decisions but how could you how could you do it. Jimmy senior just stared at me. I thought I could make it I was sure they were trampolines or nets. I mean I was so high up , I didn't know what to do. I shook that's what Tim said but why didn't you walk at that point Tim happened to come inside and say I saw Jimmy smiled at me and said he's right you should listen to him no I told him you're selfish I need you. I need you we need you. I look at the baby. I'm right here he says I always will be. Just my say my name and I'll be there, and Tim said at the same time I'm here Angela. I looked at Tim and then where Jim Sr was, and Tim's gone. I don't call him back I don't want to know. I go into the kitchen instead and grab a bottle of wine. Tim just stands looking at me as I took the wine and go upstairs with the baby. And the next day is 9/11. I watch the news and you could almost forget that it was his birthday. I didn't want to do anything. How could I have a grief and we're in the middle of a war and everything was a mess but Time Marches on at least that's what my mom told me. Even the news was talking about him I forgot, and they said the one shade of happiness we have today will give you more on the 11:00 News. True to the word they were there they came out. The cameras were there. Thank God for Tim. I got the cake he told me it was coming at 2:00 I'll be back to help set up for the party should be in time for the news cameras and he was, he was back in time. We all stood together my mom his parents, Jen, Dylan and a few other kids Chris and Kelly from school they were all there and the cameras. Jimmy didn't know he just put his face in the cake and made a mess we got some good pictures and I looked around and I thought from a distance I saw Jimmy senior in the tree.

TIM

Yeah, I knew that Jimmy's first birthday was going to be tough, and it was tough on me too, but you know it distracted me. It gave me something to do and I'd like to keep busy everyone knows that about me. Don't call me the busy Beaver for nothing. You know. So, I really enjoyed it and of course the bonus was I got to be there for the kids and for Angela. I know she needed someone, and I know she liked that I was there, and I was going to be her Rock. I didn't want to step in I know she had to grieve, and I really was just trying to be a friend. But still, I'm not going to lie. In the back of my mind, I must have known I loved her and that I wanted a good relationship with her, but I was just going to let it play out nothing happened that was okay too. I just got to be there for the kids and her. I had a feeling I didn't know it was going to take ten years but that's okay she was my Sally, and I was her Harry. Eventually it was going to happen. Wasn't waiting mind you I was just living. Biggest day is when Dylan told her that he wanted to play football. I don't think he's ready for that. She even got mad at him when he said he talked to the coach. I tried to calm him down and again when he said that he talked to the coach. It's too dangerous I went to Dylan and said and whispered to him and said I got this. Dylan went outside and I just stood with her, and she said I can't not yet it's too dangerous and I said look give it a try just let it go a few days if it's too much you'll know. She looked at me and said wow. Jim would have wanted it I said sure then do it do it for Jim.

Angela looks at me and not he tells me thank you for being there for me.Angela Everything Tim did for the birthday I knew it was time it's almost a year and I knew I would never forget it to me but still, and so I went up to the Attic and got some suitcases and boxes and put all this stuff in and then drag it back up to the Attic I didn't throw it away. I knew the kids might want to see it someday, but I didn't need it in the closet anymore now it's time to put the past to the past and try to move on. Oh, sure for Tim yet but the whole time that I was up in the attic I knew Jim was watching me. I knew he was standing but I said I must do it and he said I know and even Jimmy Junior ,we were all there we are proud of her. I'm staring at me, and I say it's time I'm not throwing it away though I'm saving it for you guys. They look through some of the stuff and I asked him did you save her stuff, and he knows it's in the Attic too. You never know he says it's true you never know. So, I kept it in the attic, and we all came down and I said goodbye to Jim, and we ate my spaghetti meatballs and garlic bread and we laughed for the first time in a long time we laughed It felt good. I looked at Jimmy Jr and said you are like him though you know that and you get that same look on your face when you're happy, when you're joking around that he always got. It's true I'm not him. I know I'm just letting you know you remind me, and Jimmy walked out. Tim just said sometimes they don't want to know. I looked at everyone and I said it's going to be okay, and I went upstairs, and I hugged him, and I said I promise I won't do that anymore baby and he hugged me. It's not that I don't want it to, it just it hurts so much. Mommy I never knew him and I said I know if you ever want to know a story just tell me and I'll let you know it's time .The past is the past but he's always there and always be in your heart and in my heart and he said I know I feel him too and I said I know you always have because you're like him doing things and he drives hard but you are so much him and I have Jimmy and I said but enough of this let's go laugh again .What should we tell them ?You want to go for a ride? All of us. You pick the spot any place, Chuck e cheese and so we all go to Chuck e cheese and play video games and laugh.

Present

Jen

I was so mad that day I found out that they were moving in together. I did not like it one bit sure I was older now, but I didn't want to forget about Mom. He said that he told her not to go into work that day and they fought about it, and she wouldn't she just went upset with her too and I know that's not fair to be upset with her too. I can just imagine my dad running into a phone booth, trying to get a hold of her from work telling her to leave and he found out, but he couldn't save her. Dad said he would call her and say please don't go babe please stay home and don't worry I'll pick the kid up I'll pick up the kid and he did but still it was a horrible disaster. I miss Mom but at least it wouldn't be the two of us and all the sadness. Dad says he saw the planes hit the towers.

JIMMY JR

Dylan often tells me how perfect the family was before I was born . I think he told me this because he knows I was the 9/11 baby and I got so much attention. I think he was jealous but he'll never admit that. He's a great big brother but none the less he does make me sad, when he tells me before your burn we were the cleavers Mike Ward and June and me and then you came. Yeah baby made three I've always heard the story. I heard the story so many times I want to scream. This is usually when he's mad at me. I tell him the story about how he was born and all the happiness and that he didn't know Dad and that makes them a little sad and guilty and I usually get what I want. I'm not saying it to get what I want one maybe a little but mostly I'm just saying the truth and I put him in his place. When I was born there watching David Letterman then mom's water broke and dad was laughing about some stupid joke David Letterman was talking about on the top 10. When he was born everyone's crying in the TV was blaring and mom was alone. I was 9/11 kid but what the heck does that really mean. I know what they want it to mean...but...I wish I knew him I really do you know what I could get away with anything I really could there was just one time and I was at school I was in second grade I think I got some turtles and put them in the teacher's desk and another time I didn't even do my homework for a week when I showed up late when I was in the fourth grade. Mom is too busy grieving I'm by the time I was old enough while it was too late . At least there was Tim he was always present you know. He was a great dad. So I had him to cover for me the teachers would always say well I'll tell your mom that was like like she really cares just tell Tim. First it was fun you know I got to do whatever I wanted to do but after a while sometimes it was a challenge. It's like how much can I do until my mom notices. It's always Tim that helps me out of the jams I got myself into it school. Just so you know it's not that I didn't love my Mom don't get me wrong she was just grieving. I know that but I don't know how you get over everything that happened thank you can. So I understand where Mom is coming from I would probably be a hot mess if it was me. But you know when she finally did snap out of it she made up for it and I got a great dad.

DYLAN

As bad as Jimmy Junior thinks he had it I think I had it worse. I mean yeah I knew my dad and to lose someone just like that with the snap of a finger and then this new baby comes along. And for this to happen all at once it would have been a big enough problem is Dad that live but without dad taking me a little love with the new baby I was thrown under the bus right away. Also do not forget that Mom was checked out.That only made matters worse. I was seven when dad died. It wasn't until I was 15 that things got really bad. At 15 that's when I started to drift. But at least I had Jennifer she was my savior and we have a lot in common and she was my sweetheart. We went to all the dances together and we went to prom and sometimes we even skip school. I mean he was the only one who could really understand . She lost her mom and I lost my dad and that kind of thing I think really Bonds you . I knew when I was having a bad day all I have to do is look at Jennifer and she got it. There's something that can be stressed without words and only someone who's gone through what you can I understand that. So like I said by the time high school came around Jen and I we were bonded tight. When we did skip school we didn't do anything bad we just had to you know get away sometimes we go to Coney Island and sometimes we'd go to the Statue of Liberty and just take the boat around. No one really seemed to care. It's amazing we got away with what we did .For instance Jen and I Drive to the Statue of Liberty no one even asks us what we're doing we would just drive and Park and this one day we just parked the car .I wanted to go to Coney Island But Jen said no way and said let's go to the Statue of Liberty and so we did. The city was our escape. Two times we would just drive to the city to get away . In the city we can just blend in and no one really cared. I think it was our happy place. And like I said I really wanted to go get a Coney dog and ride the ferris wheel but I could tell that Jen was in the zone and she really needed to think. So we went to the Statue of Liberty and got on the boat and I grab the lighter and let her cigarette. I remember like it was yesterday I got a big smile on her face and then I hug her and she smiles and she tells me I am a savior.

JEN

Yeah he was my savior without him I wouldn't have survived. I think what I remember about that day was the waiting all the waiting ..all of us all waiting waiting waiting and that's all I can think about , when I as I stare at the Statue of Liberty that day I remember too I was having trouble with school and just got my period and that's why I didn't want to go to Coney Island I just need to think. Of course I didn't tell him about my period but he was crying you could tell . I just needed to brood between the past and now.

We got in the ferry and I stared and it was great it's amazing and I snuggled into Dylan and he kissed me and that was the beginning of our romance. I felt safe with him and I know he felt safe with me. I know it seems weird with our parents married and all that but they weren't yet they were barely friends and we didn't know but no one said anything I guess they were too busy grieving anyway. I guess it wasn't destined to be a romance forever but I'm glad I had what I had and I got to love him and he supported me through the worst of the years and that day was bad but it was good too. Not often did I feel safe. That day I did my day was amazing. I didn't want to think of anything but as I looked at the sky all I could see was ten years ago and all I could think about is what my daddy was doing ten years ago . We looked at the New York skyline where the world trade center should have been, but wasn't. As I stare at the skyline I see my mommy and I close my eyes and I imagine what she would say to me.

Kathy

Honey I know you're sad. I know it's hard. Wish I could be there for you this day the day you started your period. Give you tampons and pads and let you choose and tell you this is a big day that you're a woman now. I would take you out for food and tell you now you had to be careful and you would laugh say mother . And I would say I know you're too young for all this now but you won't be always just promise me you'll come to me. I was robbed of all that you were only a baby when I died and these are the things that I wanted to tell you.

Jen

I open my eyes now and I just see the water. I tell my mother thanks for the advice and I appreciate it more now. I know she's here for me the best that she can be. I Comfort her and tell her that we weren't robbed of anything because she's here she's here for me and as I stare out into the the water I cry.

I'll never forget that night. Grandma picked me up we drove in silence.

As I waited in the yard of the playground I felt my mom. I was only seven but I knew something wasn't right. Just stood over me and watch me. I knew she was giving me strength and I told her I loved her and she told me she loved me and that it was time to go but that she would always love me. I was Seven but I knew. They didn't think I knew but I remembered. To this day I remember going into the house all dark and I wondered where Mom was, and I was scared because the house wasn't supposed to be dark. Mom got home late sometimes but not this late and where was Dad, but I didn't ask. These things because at seven I knew I wasn't going to get any answers. That was just the way it was. My grandma started humming then I started humming and we started giggling and laughing and we went in the house and Grandma turned on the lights and everything is okay because Grandma was humming Grandma would not be humming if everything wasn't okay. Right.? I remember walking into the house and Grandma placed the radio loud and we danced crazy we danced for like twenty minutes, forever it seems like and when we finally stopped dancing, we were hungry. Grandma goes to the kitchen and Grandma looks in the fridge and pulls out some macaroni and heated it up and I start to eat, and Grandma starts to eat and we're almost laughing. There's a noise Grandma looks out the window nervously I can't help but notice it's just the neighbor she says, and we go back to eating but it's not the same. Then there's a noise again. This time it was Daddy. I run into Daddy's arms, and he tries to smile even though he's dirty and exhausted. I slept and I asked where Mommy was, and he looks sad. Grandma says all right it's time for bed and I'm not and get to bed and go away. I let Grandma guide me to bed as daddy eats his cold spaghetti. There's a noise and I jump out of bed and see Dylan coming home to a dark house just like I did, and I know. Daddy's looking out the window too and I was right. I run downstairs and I peek and I see him staring out and I wonder thinking what was he thinking. I run back to the window and see Dylan going in.

DYLAN

Sitting there watching Jen . I thought of that September Day and how long it took for my grandma to pick me up. My grandma finally picked me up. It was late when I got home but grandma said Mommy was having the baby when we got home it was dark. I've never been out that way, but I was excited because I was having a baby brother and I thought dad was there that's why I was forgotten. I didn't really know, or I didn't want to know. I wasn't a dummy at five. I think I just didn't want to think about it. I looked across and saw Jennifer looking out the window and I quickly looked away and started following my grandmother. Dinner that night was simple leftovers. I was just dancing around and screaming I'm going to get a baby brother. I'm going to have a baby brother and Grandma smiled. Brave I know she must have been crying for my dad. And I would have been, I don't know how she held it together. I do remember asking Grandma or rather Grandma telling me that mom had the baby that I was having a baby brother and I was super excited. When she told me it was a boy, I was like like Daddy she said his name is Jimmy Jr and I smiled that's Daddy's name and she smiled again, and I ate my mac and cheese happy as a clam knowing I was getting a baby brother and his name was Jimmy. I heard a noise and I said Mommy and she said no and looked out the window and I saw Tim staring out. Then I look back and I saw my dad staring at me and I said Daddy and grandma looked at me and shook her head. Knew what she thought and I've tried to tell her I saw my dad but she wouldn't listen. Stood that's how older people were. But I still told my dad how much I love him and I feel comfort to know that he was there. Even though no one told me yet I knew.

Past

TIM

I was worried sick about the kids I knew they went to the city they didn't know that I knew .

The city was a scary place and when I thought of this city all I thought of the smoke massive smoke and no one can see anything so it's amazing the kids actually likes to me because when I think of it everyone's dazed and confused watching The towers fall and I'm on the ground looking up through the rebels digging digging and trying to put fires out cuz who knows what was going to happen before social media no one knew anything and I grab the water as it gets darker and darker and look at my watch it's dirty and I see it is 7:00 or 8:00 and I know I should pick up Jen but I don't. I can picture her sitting in the yard looking at the grass and teacher looking at her watch I barely get to pay phone and tell my mom to pick her and she does. If I blame anyone, I blame myself for how Jennifer turned out salty and I wasn't paying attention I mean even though nothing bad is happening I was still grieving for a lost life. I know I should have paid more attention to the kids and then there was Angela sure I paid a little too much into her, but it wasn't like that it. It wasn't like I was choosing my daughter over her or vice versa. It was more well... How can I say this, I guess I was just stuck mourning? I'm not knowing how to get through this let alone help a daughter. I knew what she was doing. I just felt powerless, and I thought I should let her alone. After all she lost her mother, and I didn't know what to do about that. How do you help a girl? I'm just going through everything I thought to myself well at least I have Angela to help just a little bit not that she could help much she couldn't even help her own kids. I did most of the heavy lifting. Oh, sure I was there I cooked dinner, but I wasn't there emotionally. I didn't know how to help a girl. I feel better around Jimmy or Dylan tossing a ball around and that's the only time I got mad. I got mad at Kathy for going into work that day for not being sick, for leaving me to raise my teenage daughter. What the hell do I know about it she's supposed to be with her, and I was supposed to have the weekends sort of be a Disney dad. Yeah, and that's how it was supposed to work out, but it didn't. I did the best I could, and I know it wasn't good enough but look how she turned out. Look what she became. When I look back, I think it was good enough. I mean no one knows what to do for someone who lost their mother and that alone in the grand scale of things was what it was.

Present

JIMMY JR

Dylan was my hero I guess that's normal for most little brothers to say that. Though I did hate him just a little bit. Here he was good at anything. He was good at sport he was good at writing and most of all he knew dad. He was perfect. Yeah, I know looking back in hindsight he was not so much perfect, and he had his issues right. Yeah, we all did. I was not Jealous of him okay well maybe a little bit but still.... I loved him a lot. He is my big brother okay. But there was this little part of me that I wanted to play football in high school, and I saw the pictures of him with Dad and I was like this isn't fair.

I know he was trying to follow in Dad's footsteps, but I had no footsteps to follow in and mom was just a mess for the first 10 years, and you know according to child development the first two years is what really makes you. If that's true I should be a hot mess. I mean it's not true because I am now a big football, I mean soccer player star. If it's true that the first couple years form you then I should not be where I am. I mean I know my mom loved me and she held me, and she didn't abuse me, and I had Tim around thank God, so I guess I mean I did for the most part have that love. But there's still something that I was craving. I wanted what dly had. I mean Tim was not a sports guy. I know you would think he was, but he wasn't. And anyway, it wasn't the same I heard all the stories about how daddy Jimmy would go out with Dylan and play sports with him and catch ball and I didn't have that I mean Tim was too busy with Jen and I don't think I ever saw him throw a ball ever. And of course, to hear mom talk about it she really didn't even want Dylan to play, and it wasn't even an issue for me to throw a ball around because way too many memories, to see Tim throwing a ball with me. God forbid that would have made mom cry. I was stuck.

I guess having dad die, not that I wish he wasn't there, but that took me on a different path. I got to play soccer .I got to find my own path. Then I wouldn't have wanted to, and I didn't want to play football but mind you just wasn't in the cards. I didn't get to be that normal All-American boy. Playing football or baseball with his dad. I know weird right you think I would have been that all American boy according to all the magazines, but I wasn't, not by a long shot. Don't believe everything you hear. Then of course there were the times that Dylan was made to play with me. I knew he really didn't want to0 and I know Mom made him, but you know what it still made me happy. And still hear mom's voice saying go throw a ball with them giving Dylan a sideway glance. When I would just whine so much about having nothing to do or know where to go or no one to play with. I know what you wanted to say your dad would have and just like that Dylan he felt guilty. That we didn't have fun I just knew his heart wasn't in it and so I didn't whine too much. But he did have fun and I did learn some things.

I know what Mom saw when she saw us playing, I know she saw Jimmy senior daddy Jimmy. If she did, she hid it well.

I could tell because I saw a little tear in her eye, and I knew that tear and I meant she was remembering but she was having a bad moment often when that happened Tim would run out to play with us and mom would smile. But Tim had his own issues why he couldn't play he had his inhaler from all the smoke on 9/11 and Tim would start coughing and then Jen would come running and say Daddy are you okay and just as easily as the game got started it was over. Usually then Dylan would say hey babe watch me, and Jen would smile and forget all about her dad and sneak a kiss no one saw. But I always did, and I would just shake my head. So The most I ever got was like a few minutes of catch before all heck would break loose that's okay I started just kicking a soccer ball around on my own learning how to hit it with my head and I watched a lot of soccer movies and then I tried out the moves I was getting pretty good and I could see Mom smiling sometimes from the windows she did the dishes so I know I entertained her and that was good too.

ANGELA

I would watch everyone from the window as I cleaned up the dishes. And I would see Jimmy Jr sneak off the soccer ball I was happy for him but still I would get a little upset because I would wonder what Jim would think. Usually right about then Tim would come up to me look at me and say it's okay for him to be good at something that his dad wasn't. You know his dad would have wanted that. And I would look at Tim and sigh and say I know and then Tim would throw a little bubble on me or make me laugh and forget for a minute and I would laugh at the thought of Jimmy Jr bouncing balls off his head. No idea he was going to be a big star people ask me all that all the time and I said he was just a kid just playing, surviving. I'm glad for those nights those nights made me happy because of what held me together. I'm glad for Tim especially. And always though in the corner of my eye I would see the gym watching his boy and he would smile, and I knew it was okay and sometimes he would wink at me, and I know he was okay with me and Tim. Even still I found a little bad all the way around.

JEN

It wasn't so much the early years that had me troubled. It was my teenage years as strange as that sounds the early years were so easy it was when I was a teenager that I really suffered I think it was because I realized what was going on. I didn't want to be special I didn't want to think about it losing my mom I just wanted to blend in. But I couldn't I couldn't forget they're always photographing us asking us questions about 9/11 as soon as someone found out I lost the parent during 9/11 they'd always talk to me and and so I learned not to say anything. Now I can talk about it then I just wanted to forget for a few years. I wanted to be a cheerleaderband just being a normal teenager. I just wanted to pretend I know that's impossible now but just for a little bit I would forget and I could be a giggly girl. But when I came back to reality I.

Every moment was bad oh no I mean there was homecoming there was Christmas dances there was football games and of course prom. Always wonder what my mom would think would she have wanted me to wear a rose colored dress would we have fought over what lipstick to wear I wanted to wear leather and she said no I thought of those things and I'm glad that I had Angela it made it a little easier but still I thought of my mom and how we'd fight it out. Angela never really fought with me I guess she felt like she couldn't she had to wear baby gloves so to speak. Yes I'm glad as close as we were I'm glad that she treated me like that cuz I probably would have yelled and screamed you're not my mother. I'm glad I didn't have to say any of that you know. Through high school I just got to be. I had three years to grow and change finally in my senior year I was ready and Dylan and I had a blast we are both able to forget just for a little bit. I wish though that I had my mom to talk to as much as I liked Angela at the time I know she had her own problems and it wasn't the same and sometimes I felt a little guilty.But still I wish I could tell her about doing that I met the cutest boy that I was going to prom with him and that he was my first. I know what my mommy Kathy would say. I knew by then she was the no-nonsense type. She would have put my hands on her and smiled at me and said I'm glad you found someone but be careful baby. Late at night when I'm lying alone tucked in bed I imagine her by my bedside.

KATHY

So darling what would you like to talk about tonight. So who's this boy doing I heard you talk about to one of your friends. I saw his name in your notebook you know the one that you wrote All over. Tell me is he cute? Tell me does he make you go Gaga. I know it's embarrassing baby but you can tell me anything. Has he asked you yet to prom, don't worry he will. Just promise me when he does you'll tell me everything. We'll go out and buy a red dress and we'll get your hair done and your nails and I have the perfect shoes for you.

JEN

And she fades away. My mom is a girly girl, she would have loved getting me ready for prom.

I was not at that point as girly as I could have been and I know with my mom's influence she would have made me girly. Would have installed the love of shopping in me . I sigh . And hug my blankets just a little bit closer to me imagining what you would say and seeing her in the shadows actually quietly walks away.

DYLAN

Our prom was special, and I still have the song I wrote for her. Sweet sweetie nothing smiles, sweet nothings in my ear. Not special but everything special at the same time nothing will be the same but the more it changes the more it stays the same and it's true. I still have the paper I wrote it on. Someday I should do something about it write it into a full song. That night was the best I've ever had regardless of everything that's happened in between. I'll never forget how she made me feel. I know we became a couple that didn't last. You know we were young even if they had not become a couple, mom and daddy Tim, I don't think we would have last. We had to find ourselves and it just didn't last mom and Tim were supportive they never said a peep. They wouldn't have minded that we lost our virginity to each other. They really wouldn't have minded but somethings you just must keep to yourself. For sure it came out later and we left it. I think they knew anyway but they didn't make a big deal out of it. We just ate dinner that night and they asked how prom was and we said fine, and I squeezed her hand and that was it. They themselves a look which I noticed, and Jen did too, and Tim winked at mom but that was it. An end to a perfect night to a perfect year really. And then I spent the rest of the time looking at pamphlets for Stanford like I had planned. I had to get out of the area.

You are beauty you're eternal, I tell Jen you're a life itself sometimes I miss him but when I see you smile it all goes away, I'm lean into Jennifer and kiss her I love you I say, and the answer is in the wind Jen looks at me and tells me I'm the best. You're a great writer you know that right. I look away and stare at the water. It doesn't matter Jen tells me. I tell her I'm going to his school and playing football and she tells me f them it's your life I throw a rock into the ocean and watch it go out into the horizon yeah f him .I say I'll go to Berkeley and study writing and you will come out and live with me and it'll be awesome. I put my hand on Jennifer's and we make out until security guard comes just as I am putting my hand on her boobs. Her hands on my crotch but she managed to get a kiss in anyway and I touch her, and security guy says that's it lights out last call last very and we go. We leave the statue of liberty. I know what my dad would have thought my daddy Jimmy but the whole prom and the promise ring he would have been all guy guy and just winked at me and smiled and said go for it kid. Just like Jen late at night in the kitchen it's like grab a sandwich I see my dad.

JIMMY SR

Hungry son ? That's not how you make a sandwich you got to put more meat on that buddy. No problem was did you get lucky? Was she good! ! The first time isn't as good don't worry about it, it will only get better don't worry. I bet you got that same spirit the same Italian you know spirit that your old dad has. I bet you were wicked on the dance floor were you not and I bet you danced like this. Hey don't laugh at your dear old dad buddy. I may be out of touch but I still know how it works . Seriously hey before you go to bed sit down tell me a little bit more I know you're a teenager but you can tell me. Tell me everything don't be a man of few words.

DYLAN

And I told dad everything. Well not quite everything. I was a Teenager after all but he understood and offered me Father knows Best wisdom. I just told him she was great and yeah I kick butt on the dance floor. And that smiled and said I knew you would you got that from your old man kiddo keep it up. It turned off the light and said don't stay up too late ain't that sandwich and won't tell your mama thing just get to bed kid. And he disappeared into the night. He always disappeared but that's what Dad did, right !?

ANGELA

Don't think Tim and I didn't know we knew what they did. I just didn't make a big deal out of it. Fine by Us. After prom then it was graduation every parent's bittersweet happy ending. Proud of our kids not wanting to move on and at least we still have Jimmy Jr. Graduation was great it all happened in such flurry the party's the fun it was amazing. And Jen she was a little lady and accepted her diploma beautifully with Grace and Dylan of course he was Mr. Cool and class clown he had to wink it me and Tim and then ran up and grabbed his diploma and that was the worst of it but no Mr. dignified he thought he would do worse but he just smiled and oh and he did pull down his shorts but everyone laughed he sort of did a flash but it was nice I think there was some photographers but that was it was only one magazine article written. That was just all about how the kids were growing up now and what were they going to do and what the future was. Nothing compared to when Jimmy Jr graduated but by then we were used to it and so was Jimmy. But after graduation we partied, and we had fun all of us and with their friends and it was a great summer and really was. At the party it was the last time I saw Jimmy senior. If I would have seen him when Jimmy graduated but I think I was past it. And he did tell me it was time that's his way of saying he had to go.

You smiled at me and said our boys are grown up you did a good job and I smiled back with a tear I know, and you gave a good foundation.

He smiled and with a little help from him pointing at Tim. It's true and Tim came over then and hugged me and just like that he kissed me and just like that Jim was gone. I love you I whispered, and Tim knew I was talking to him , Tim smiled, and I said I love you too. I think he's gone forever. Maybe Tim said. Intense. He worled me around the dance floor and then danced with Jen I cried a little bit it was like I was seeing everything fresh .

In ten minutes, Tim headed to the truck, and I smile and tell him I'll be right there. I see Jimmy and him and he tells me you know what you need to do right, and I nod. It's to hard I say. He tells me he knows but you must do it you made a promise you have to take care of the kids. I'm right here I'll always be here let me go he says it's time and I nod. As hard as it is I nod none the less. and that night I let him go. I look at the truck and smile my future. Of course, I never forgot Jimmy senior he's with me every day in my heart, but I knew I had to move on that night for my little boy my little miracle and there was my future. Little did I know it then, but we will get married Tim and I and have a great future. As I look at them together, I remember when Tim first held him when he was a baby. And every time since and felt thankful that he been a great dad I'm shocked to realize that's what it is. Remember all the times as much as I wanted Jim to be there it was Tim. I think I knew that all along but of course you can't admit it but that night I did I saw it all in my head and I really lived with it that he was the dad that Jimmy needed. I remember a little old lady looked at them and said it's great to see a father and son and I didn't even correct her. I just nodded and let it sit and let it sink in. Because I realized it was true. I knew he thought of it that way too.

Past

TIM

After all that fuss, I didn't know what to tell her . I was glad that she was sticking to her decision, and I was impressed. I did tell her wow when you decide you really do it and she said I know you don't know that side of me but it's true I can be a rough and tumble kind of girl if I need to be. But when it's time it's time and we're going to get counseling, I mean I need to do it for my kids we need to get back up on the horse. That's when I told her that I loved her, and I said I love you do you hear me, and we kiss, and Angela looks up at me and smiles I love you too. You don't have to say it, but I want to I need to, and I smile, and we looked up to the moon and she leaned on me my shoulder and closed her eyes and we fell asleep on the swing until I got too cold, and we went inside. we fell asleep on the couch.

Present

DYLAN

I didn't understand I was very mad at my mom and Tim for trying to have a relationship. I miss my dad. Not till about sixteen do I realize that my mom deserves love too and that of course she missed my dad. But then I was bonded with Tim, and he really was like a father figure, and I know I owed him the world. I had long forgiven my mom. Not that she needed for giving you know. I did and that's when I realized parents are only human too. I know my mom talked to Jimmy senior and so did Jimmy not me. I just slept with my helmet on when I was little so not to forget. I did over time you know I started to forget. And that night I was mad I was mad enough to slam my door and I looked at my window and saw Jen and then a few minutes later I saw Tim walk across the lawn and I heard Mom's window bedroom door shut. She slipped into my room where I was already in bed pretending to be asleep. I want her to know. That I knew that would come later. I really didn't understand them, and I didn't want to understand. All I know is he wasn't my dad and that wasn't her husband. If I had been younger, I would have screamed he's not my father, but I wasn't and I didn't. That night changed everything it really did it made me grow up just a little bit because it's something that made me realize when I grow older, and I looked back that life is different. I fell asleep and when I woke up Mom is cooking pancakes it was like a whole different mom, she told me and Jimmy we were going to summer camp. I just looked at her like who are you and she smiled and said camp starts in two weeks I was amazed at all the differences in my mom that morning. I wasn't looking forward to camp I wasn't going to fight her, and I knew then that was not the time to say anything I knew about her and Tim if I felt like there was a light in her. And I didn't want that to go away. I did challenge for a little bit though. I said not just the both of us just for him and she shook her head confirming what I already knew. I frowned you got to be kidding me. I screamed I don't want to go I'm too old. She just frowned and said look you'll have fun you need to deal with the the grief. There's a honk and I see Jen and I run outside, and Jen and I drive away. Riding off into the sunset. but still not far away enough to forget our problems and to push all the dread away. As we leave, I see Tim crossing into the driveway of our house. I frown but we don't stop.

Past

TIM

I see the kids drive away and I walk into the house. Smile at Jimmy Jr and rub Angeles shoulders. Angela frowns. I look at Angela and say well I guess they didn't take it too well. And tell by the look on Angela's face. What I just said was an understatement.

So, I rub her shoulders more and tell her it's better late than never you know. They'll like it maybe I'll even send Jen there and she laughs. Jimmy jr looks happy though. I Had the desired effect I've made her feel better. It's only momentarily though. I don't think all the drinking I've done in the past can make up for anything she says. I just rub her shoulders again and tell her we can't help it. We've been through a lot too. They will understand when they are older. Angela nods. I knew from history from Dylan from what he told me that she did this a lot, so I didn't ask too many questions. I just sat there and hope this was a time where she wouldn't give in that she would be there for me for the family. We were trying to build. I don't want to watch things, but I knew it was time and I hope she really did.

ANGELA

Telling Jimmy and Dylan about the camp was not my best moment. They're very upset and I knew I could never make up for it. They weren't Dylan was. Jimmy was glad I think he was going to be glad to get away. But I was devastated with Dylan's thoughts and reaction, but I let him go. Glad Tim is there to make me feel better because all I could think about was all the time, I let Dylan down all the times I wasn't there for him, for his performances, his games and trips. I didn't know how to make things better. And wasn't as bad he just ran out and glared at me other times, he's played his music loud fought me yell at me curse me throwing stuff even. At least I knew he was safe he was with someone who would come back and get him back here for that I'll always be grateful. Jimmy senior was around he would have told me just let him go and he would have laughed saying like me, but he has your temper. Completely 100% true he does look like him too. All the times I didn't see Tim for what he was because Jimmy senior got in the way. This time I wasn't going to let that happen. I gave into the urge of wanting to kiss Jimmy sooner and tell him everything. I meant it a new me was brewing. Anyway, he was there but I had to be in the moment and let everything be. It was time and he deserved it. I deserved it and the kids deserved it

JEN

I looked at Dylan next to me. I'm trying to comfort him. I told him, people could be counselors and he just shrugged. I didn't press it any longer. I just let him have all his motions yell and hit.

But I've seen it all and he did all that again and finally he looked at me and said talking helps. I said I know I rolled my eyes and kiss Dylan and don't smile. He managed to laugh and started to sing, maybe she can find you one that you can do that in that way that could be groovy. He shrugged now she wants me to go to a camp that's all about grief. Then I shrugged and said there's all different kinds of grief you know. Different ways to handle stuff and we both just looked at each other.

DYLAN

Before camp we had a lot to do at school. They are coming to us to interview US as it's been 17 years. Being on all the covers of the magazines talking about what 9/ 11 means and where we were at now. We went to school looking our best our Sunday best and Jen in her cheerleader outfit me and my football gear look like the prom queen and king that we were. Jen looking at the camera and then runs out and I run after her asking her what's wrong. She just shrugs Just smiles and talks to her gals and does a split in the hallway and says that's how it's done kids. All confidence that is the Jen I knew. And I kiss her right there in the hallway and everyone looks at us. We are the couple. We are the moment and I know the place she's at. But you know not everything is as it seems deep down of course we all know there's a lot of grief even though Jen cheers and I play football and smile. We were teenagers what do you expect. I mean there is mental health issues no matter what you know they're all watching us play. They all expect us so happy. They forget we're just kids. But mom and Tim stand watching us with little Jimmy who's having a blast. I'd rather be singing, expressing my pain, but I hide it well.

JIMMY JR

I would goof around at home I didn't take it seriously enough I would just watch the soccer players at the park or wherever. Till one day Kelly came up to and said I noticed you, you are good. Want to play. I said no. I'm a football guy. She just shook her head and said whatever suits you. Let me know if you want to kick the ball around and finally, I thought what the heck and I got involved. Even though they were a little older than me, I still managed to kick some ass so yeah, I was always pretty good not to toot my horn but once I get going there was no stopping me. I was a lean mean fighting machine. Kelly told me after I was pretty good, and I said thanks and I must have hesitated too long because she said yeah, my parents always trying to make me into something I'm not too you know. I nodded glad that someone understood. Dylan really didn't talk much about it. Kelly and I never really talked about it after that, but we were just playing she became my outlet someone I could trust.

JEN

It's true what they say senior year is the best year ever. I had the most fun even though I knew I was going to have to go to that camp and I was going to have less time with Dylan. I still was happy. And after my senior play there was prom and Dylan looks so cute in his outfit and his talks and we dance, and he brought me a corsage and it was amazing. I just sped up; I wish I could have slowed time down. But you know what it' like okay time never does what you wanted it to do. There was the best time of my life just like that song from dirty dancing. It indeed was the time of my life. And to top it all off I was prom queen and Dylan was prom King. It was so magical. Such great memories. I know people looked at us they want we were perfect, and I guess in a way we were but, in the inside, we were just a little bit damaged. Later we would go crazy in college finding myself but now I was in delusions and having fun. It's not fair to say I was in delusions I wasn't I just wasn't dealing with reality. That's not fair either it's more than that. I just got lost in the moment and had fun and everything was meant to be. I thought it would last with dly. It didn't matter that mom and he were together it's not like we are real brother and sister. We weren't really at all. And I wanted dly to be the first because he meant so much to me so that night after prom we got together, and we lost our virginity. It was special they say the first time must be special and this was not just because it was prom because it was him because we've grown up together because we meant so much and we really did think we were going to be together forever. You never know what the future will hold but dly always has a special spot in my heart. He told me love me that night and I told him. And we meant it. I woke up the next morning and joked around and nothing was bad and said good morning and I said good morning and we did it again forever I said forever he said. Then he got out his guitar and started playing. He asked if he was good well, he played around on the guitar, and I nodded, and he broke out in song. Same for me

He gives me a promise ring that night and it made me happy and made the whole night beautiful and real and I said yes. This night is perfect now and we danced off into the night under the stars with the soft music I knew that night our future was entwined . It didn't matter. Nothing mattered then. Looking back on it now I realized all that mattered was the moment. I thought we would and I know if I could go back in time and tell myself we didn't I would say it doesn't matter and I wouldn't even want to. I wouldn't want to take that perfect moment and throw it away . Life gives you so little perfect moments you know and so it was perfect it was amazing.

A kiss and he smiled, and I knew he meant forever too, it wasn't just forever it was forever. Dylan, I meant it too. I really did . I took all the Care in the world to get that ring. That night was magic. I don't care what else happened. The night was real, and magic doesn't come around that much. Live the magic and before they whisked us off to camp or at least her we had a great few weeks. I could feel them staring at us they weren't mad just perplexed. I know they thought we were too young, but I didn't care it was just a promise ring, but it was so much more, and I know that's why we were just off at camp to see if I love would survive it like Danny and Sandy . I knew it would. I tell my mom about the promise ring and I tell her that they want to send me to camp. She's all sympathetic and says she understands. And she's happy about the promise ring and that she knows Dylan and I will be happy forever after unlike her and my dad. Exactly what I need to hear after my dad is so mean to me it's making me to go to camp making me not want to be with Dylan thinking we're too young.

KATHY

Oh my God that ring is beautiful Jen. We get it I know it's not quite the engagement ring we had wished but it's one step closer isn't it. Going to get through this whole camp thing don't worry about it your dad's just trying to break you up you know. I'm the good cop and he's the bad cop. Don't sweat it just remember you have forever with Dylan he's your forever guy ,don't let your dad take that away.

JEN

I smile and say thanks Mama. As she walks away. Glad someone has my back and all this and that's all I need. She just made my day and now I can get on with my life and my day knowing that it's all going to be okay. Dad is the bad cop and Mom is my savior. I know that's what I made it out to be. It's true that's what I made it up to be but now I love my dad and I would give anything for more time with him. Daddy I whisper I'm sorry.

Present

DYLAN

Like Jen if I could go back in time and tell my younger self I don't even know if I would because all the magic and all the songs that came out of that and not really sorrow there was no sorrow it was just love. You never forget true love and it's true. She became a movie star and I became a writer neither of us married , I don't think that's because we are holding a candle to each other still . I think it's just because we're too busy being and living.Just wish could tell my younger self hey it's going to be okay. I wish I had daddy Jimmy to let me know that he loved me. That he was proud of me. I know what he would say about the ring.

Jimmy Sr

You dog you. Where'd you get the ring bud. Let me see it. Cool I'm very proud of you kid. Remember forever's a long time but if this is what you want I'm supporting you 100%. Anyone talk you out of it okay I'll talk to your mom bud and we'll make it all right.

DYLAN

Yeah I know that's what Dad would say. Yeah I know that's too perfect but that's what I needed and I knew that's who my dad was he was laid back and cool and groovy and and he was there for me he was like Ward from leave it to Beaver just smiled and winked and he was perfect. Jen and I knew they would understand not like Tim and Angela.

Past

TIM

I saw The Ring, I saw him slip it on her and I wanted to run but Angela stopped me. Were we ever that young I said, and Angela nodded we were? Don't spoil their fun night she said, and I nodded I just said three words camp. It didn't start for three weeks but you know time is time and time is funny.

A lifetime but I knew what would happen would happen no matter what we did and so I did give them their moment their moment of pure joy to have to look back on when all the hard times happened and they would even as a parent I couldn't wave a magic wand and take all the pain away or predict what was going to happen .I just knew I wanted them to have the fun because I knew from experience life could be crap sometimes. Caught up in the magic of things I kissed her I kissed Angela and Angela was taking back surprise, but she gave into it, and I twirled her around and it was amazing. Angela looked at me and smiled wondering what got into me that smile said it all. I just responded with another kiss to forget the world around us and not be parents just for one minute because life was too short.

ANGELA

That night was perfect, and the weeks flew by. Everyone had fun and before I knew it, they were off to camp and me and him were all alone for the first time ever, we're able to wake up in each other's arms and I knew this would make us or break us. We really had time to explore what would happen what we wanted. That morning alone I was looking forward to it. I didn't Wonder what was going to happen and he made me breakfast in bed all my favorite things and it was wonderful. I had no worries and we had nowhere to go it was amazing. It was truly perfect and all we had was time the summer they ahead of us like we ourselves and just graduated from high school and could explore finally our own possibility of where we were going and somehow, I knew it would all work out.

Jimmy JR

We went off to camp yes, we did we went off to camp I was twelve and dyl and Jen were seventeen and it was amazing. Me and Kelly were with the kids and Jen and Dly were with the counselors. They stuck to each other like glue for the first few weeks and even me and Kelly got stronger in fact she gave me my first kiss. I'm glad it was her.

Ever since she told me how to play soccer we were bonded. Even more I mean I was only twelve, so I didn't know where this would go if at all, but she was fourteen and an older woman and it was amazing truly amazing. As for them Dyl and Jen, I would watch them, sometimes I saw them argue and I didn't know if they would make it. I had a feeling daddy Tim and Angela knew what they were doing. I want them to be together. I had so many bad things happen at such a young age, I just I wanted some good things to happen. I was a sucker for Happy endings even then. I know everyone thought it was way too serious and I was. I always have been. Dylan he was a jokester.] He did take after Dad daddy Jim. I think. I took after Mom or maybe I got some of Tim's characteristics just by being around him but I was sulking half the time but Kelly boy she made me come alive so that did take my mind off of whatever was happening between those two and I say whatever because I saw there was a counselor that was talking to Jen and I know Dylan was a little upset but I saw him makeup so I don't know. I had no idea what was going on at home if I had known maybe I wouldn't have been so carefree but then again, I'm happy so maybe I would have but I'm glad I didn't.

TIM

I went to many stores, and I finally found the one ring I was looking for after weeks of home cooked food and lounging in bed and nothing to worry about I finally knew I was going to give her a ring it wasn't going to be a promise ring either. The time and besides I knew I wanted forever and ever. I finally found the ring I wanted in an antique store. Old diamond ring that looks like it been from the twenties it was amazing, and it made me smile and I knew she would like it too. And she did I had the perfect night planned. I know you're thinking I move fast but hey when you're older you must and plus it wasn't like we are some newbies we were going at a snail's pace we have ten years and so don't criticize me. No, you know besides. I just cooked dinner for her that night and had champagne and went to the kitchen and came out with a ring box and I gave it to her and put it on her ring finger and she smiled. Said yes. Then she ran out the door and I was left standing there wondering what just had happened.

ANGELA

I looked at the ring as I flew out the door and drove fast, I drove into to the city. And just stared into space until I got into the 9/11 memorial. And I talked to Jim as if he was there and asked him if he was okay with this. I told him I hadn't gone looking for it and I know he knew that too. I know I said he never came to me again but this time he didn't it was me coming to him and I know he whispered in my ear it's okay. I told him I loved him, and I always would but I thought it was time and he smiled and said I know I I love you too. I smiled and it was as if he was giving me to Tim giving his permission and I was okay I was happy. I drove and I could feel him watching me and waving I looked back and blew him kisses and he was gone and that was okay because I knew he'd always be watching over me and I knew he was happy. Finally, I made it back home and Tim smiled at me, and I said yes, I will, and he looked at me relieved and give me a good big kiss. I said it all and I said it's okay he gave me to you, and he smiled he understand. Where I had to go, and I knew he knew everything, and I knew then I loved him more than my heart could ever love anyone else, and I was glad that I found them, and I was glad we took it so and I was glad we were going to grow together it was totally forever. Present

JEN

I'm glad things turned out the way they did I'm not going to lie sometimes I do get sad about that last summer when I was a camp counselor and when I took Dylan's promise ring. I mean there's no guarantee that we would have made it anyway but that last summer that was intense everything was going well until about that last week of summer camp. Everyone knew me and Dylan where you know joined at the hip so to speak. Then this soccer coach started to take an interest in me, and we just started chatting innocently and then we took some walks together and he taught me how to play soccer and it started out because Jimmy you know was interested in soccer and I would just sit there watching Jimmy and the kids and he got me involved. I didn't want to be rude because he was so helpful to Jim but...

But then something switched, and it became a little flirting and after about a week or two of all this Dylan found out and I said it's no big deal probably never see him again nothing happened. I just looked at me and was like do you love him, and I was like I don't know but you're wearing my ring he said. He said look we're going away to college anyway we must explore our possibilities. You know I told him. He just got a sad look it's just a promise ring I said. Then give it back he told me. I looked at him. No just tell me he said. I do care about him. I don't know maybe I should give it back. Devastated but even more devastated because I said I didn't know but I couldn't lie I didn't want to lie. And that was it that was the end of the summer I gave him back his ring and we played it out I didn't even talk to the soccer coach but I thanked him for taking care of Jimmy and that was it and he kissed me on the cheek and I wasn't really enthused but our parents came after that and Jimmy was happy and he hugged Kelly goodbye and said he would see Kelly at school later on and he hopped in the car; I was sulky and I jumped in the car I hugged mom and I know she noticed my ring was gone but she didn't say anything. Then Dylan popped in the car, and it was awkward silence but luckily Jimmy was filling it up all about soccer and how much fun he had and how amazing it was. Except for Jimmy the road trip home was quiet. We all had our secrets, I guess.

Past

ANGELA

I had my ring in my pocket. I wasn't hiding it from the kids I just wanted to wait for the right moment, and I noticed that Jen didn't have hers and again I was waiting for the right moment.

I told him not to say a word I said it all with my eyes. Ask Jimmy questions and he was more than willing to answer anything which was good because we needed the escape. After we got home though we went out to dinner and that's where he told the kids. I was nervous and I told him we had a secret a good secret. I looked at Tim and Tim looked at me and then I just blurted it out we're engaged. And Tim said we're getting married how does people feel about that .and everyone was quiet still and then they like congratulated and got happy, but they still were a little bit sad. I could tell Jen had the sad look in her eyes, every time she looked at Dylan. Jen looked at me and asked when we were going to tie the knot and I said I'm thinking 9/11. Perfect, perfect the kids echoed. We have a lot to do. We got cakes, wedding dresses and people to invite and very short amount of time it'll be quiet of course. It was but we spent the next few weeks looking at magazines with cakes and everything and that filled up the time. between the time they had to go to college and 9/11 it took some of the empty away, in this way because of Dly and Jen not having fun but at least we were planning it and they didn't have to think about things.

I told Jen look you just cut it short by a few weeks and she said I know but I could have had a few more weeks but college would have been hard I said. Then we are back to planning the wedding. I'm glad that we had the time now because I got the bond with her before college, and we had a lot of fun. Tim bonded with Dylan. Jimmy too even more and for that we're all grateful. Some of the pressure was off at the end of the summer, for everybody and we really became a full family. I really bonded with Jen too. I know it wasn't easy and even though I'd known her forever I wanted to make sure she was okay about this whole thing. I made sure she knew that and helping plan the wedding really helped us Bond and she already told me she felt like I was a second mom now.

Present

DYLAN

I wasn't a hero you know my daddy Tim and daddy Jimmy both are more heroes than I ever been. Fighting fires helping people and just being up there in the towers, helping people get down. He did everything he could and that taught me a lot. That's the other reason why I wanted to go I want to be of service. I know everyone says that on 9/11 everyone was helpful and for months after people were bonded coming together and I guess I just wanted that. I wanted that experience and I got it. I became of service. That makes everybody happy up there and even now I stop and remember who I am and don't break and I remember I don't have to be that perfect person just Be. I have to say I feel the saddest for mom. She lost two loves of her life it must be hard, but she just gets out there keep turn going so proud of her and will always be there for her as she is for me. And I know she has Jimmy junior still so that'll keep her going and then she'll be able to get on with things, but she has four more years to be preoccupied with. I can't even imagine going through it twice I'm mad enough and here she is not even batting an eye. And look at Jen. I'm just glad that she has mom. Her mom Christ she is without parents so young. 9/11 took her mommy Kathy but she had me. Cheers to our mom. I should say which is great and we will always be a family no matter with angels looking after us. Angels looking out for us, on all levels and I know we'll get to where we want to be. So, we rock on. I know Jimmy Junior says that I don't know and that he has it all or something or that I had it worse, but I mean I think he had it worse because at least I knew dad. I know he thinks he's in. What would I do with the time machine? Jimmy Junior does have one thing right you want more and more. I mean if I had time machine of course I'd want more time with Dad. How can I not even though I wouldn't be the same person that you would see before you now like in frequency where I can say Dad you're going to die. I love that movie where the son gets to tell his dad everything that happened in his present. They're trying to solve a crime I guess the crime I would like to solve is them getting on the plane I would be like

Dad just to go to work and come back I know there's no guarantee that we all live happily ever after if I could make anything happen maybe I'd make them divorce so I don't lose anything. So, I still become the writer I am today that would be great. I would really like that yeah that would be the best thing to happen besides that's the reality I would choose. I don't think I need alternate realities so it's interesting to think about what would happen or what could happen. But yeah, that movie frequency gets me every time I cry so hard that's my life. Because every boy wants a father and I'm lucky enough to have him.

JEN

Thinking about everything, when I look back now that it's been twenty years and we've lost him I lost my dad I'm glad to have Angela.

But in terms of The Time Machine my parents we're going to divorced anyway but of course I'd want more time with Mama Cathy and I think what I would do is probably just fake sick , so she didn't have to go in or like Dly said just make it so they never got on the plane and trick him back and hope maybe in that reality Dylan and I would have gotten married there would be no brokenness but of course I'd still be broken cause the divorce and maybe Dylan would be too maybe in his parents would have gotten divorced even though they were the cleavers but regardless I guess I would hope that Dylan and I would get married. I mean I'm glad that he's there for me now and just is my best friend that's almost better, but I just wonder what that route reality would look like' cause as it is I can't imagine getting married to anyone that means no grandkids. Maybe Dylan will but I guess Jimmy is his best, moms best bet.

We lost another that's why I'm becoming an activist that's why I'm trying to fight for my family and when I say family, I mean the whole 9/11 family. I want everyone to have equal rights. If I had not been an actress and activist, I would have been a lawyer, but I like disappearing into other people's perfect world and sometimes not so perfect but when you're little you get to be someone else and you get to create their story and say yeah it is perfect at least it's not mine and at least it's not my story. Yeah, I'll miss my dad but I'm mad too. I think I had it easier growing up than some just knowing that my parents were going to get divorced according to Dad, but I know he wouldn't lie to me.

Besides leaving Dylan behind the other hardest part was dad getting married. I like her felt like she was replacing my mom too much time had gone by for that, it was more it was more that times I felt bad because I didn't remember my real mom.

I was very sad and I told my dad about it and he was like don't worry about it she would understand and I said I know but sometimes I don't remember her and he told me stories about her and how she would paint my nails and how she was a girly girl and how she loved me to the moon in the back and how proud she would be of me and he told me of trips that we went on it was beautiful. And Angela well she really encouraged me to do what I wanted to do, and she understood how I felt. If at times I felt sad about Mom Angela was totally on board and love me to death, but she gave me space at the same time. The worst of it is I felt like Dylan was my rock and I lost something, and I hope he felt the same way I felt like I lost my best friend.

TIM

It was a mad rush those last few weeks this summer. We all really bonded a lot with the kids and Dylan came to me and asked me a lot of questions and I got the reassure that everything was going to be okay. He was in pain he told me because he felt like he was losing his Rock with Jen because they had done everything togetherness. I told him that everything would come back around. He said he knows but it's just the weirdest thing I don't care so much about the relationship, and we've been together since we were five. And I just felt sad. I told them things have a way of working out. I Smiled and he thanked me and we continue to get ready for the wedding. There was a lot to do and before we knew it the big day was upon us and of course Dylan was my best man well joint best man Jim was too Jimmy Jr was too, and Jen was her matron of Honor. It was a great wedding. Simple ceremony. Family and my firefighter crew.

Jimmy Jr asked if I was happy. I said yeah, I'm just happy.

That isn't it.It's weird though I mean I know I've known you forever you but I often think about what if or what would have happened. I smiled and said of course, we all do, I told Jimmy Jr . And later I talked to my daughter, and I reassured her that I would not forget her mom and she told me I know but do you ever think about her she said. I said of course all the time she's in my thoughts all the time. But don't worry she's not being replaced. And Jen said I know it's just sometimes I feel sad because I don't remember her. I smiled and said I know babe, but you have nothing to worry about and she kissed me and said I know Dad we're all going to be happy, and I smiled. I coughed a little bit because even then I cough not as much but just a little bit. And I told her to go to bed we had a big day and I sat there watching the Stars talking to Kathy and said you'd be so proud and that's the first time I've done that in a long time, but it was worth that my wave saying goodbye. Angela with Jim Sr I never really had that kind of relationship but something that night made me do it and I'm glad I did I saw a twinkling shooting star and I knew it was her approving that I was doing the right thing.

JEN

So, dad and mom mommy Angela got married on 9/11 it was a beautiful ceremony it was amazing, and it was the most beautiful thing in the world. By then I had let go Mama Kathy well not letting go but I wasn't looking so hard I had found my own version of peace. No longer filled with teen angst . It was Peaceful and family oriented indeed, and it brought us all together.

Dylan and I did not talk just barely but finally by the time I left we sat down and we made up and it was like having the old Dylan back we just said well who knows what will happen I did I never got married so I never got to have him walk me down the aisle and say I would take the ring back and I didn't say I was didn't but of course I didn't but still I would call him all the time and college and he would call me and we became best of friends like brothers and sisters. Really and truly. That was the way it was meant to be we were this family unit this beautiful unit. I feel lost without him you know I feel lost without anybody and even Jimmy Jr we all came back for his high school graduation in 8 years, and I acted in plays, and I moved to LA where I became a superstar. I have my own talk show now and Dylan he's a writer and of course everyone knows about Jimmy Jr the world-renowned soccer player and Dad you're doing okay the cough got worse and he finally succumb to it a few years ago. Came together for his funeral. I mean we are part of the family anyway and we always came together but still to lose the patriarch was intense. I never got married so I never had him walk me down the aisle I don't know it won't happen now probably just a little trip to Vegas or something. But you know what... I don't need all that. My mom is amazing person and Angela is the most amazing person and if I have her and Dylan Jimmy at my wedding, I'll be fine not that that's going to happen anytime soon, I don't even have anybody, so I don't know what I'm talking about. I just mean I wouldn't want to have a wedding without Daddy. But that aside every time 9/11 happens I still cry I mean here we are we lost another one this one was 15 years later but it's still a 911 casually it still happening and now 20 years later now we've had the withdrawal of Afghanistan and 13 more dine very sad. Also, intense and I know this on 9/11 I'll feel it even more. I'll feel the ghosts . I'm glad they told the president not to come he did Injustice to my dad to Kathy too and Jim Sr and more. Everything should not have been that way no sir. Our family has survived worse and will survive this and I'm sure there'll be other stuff that will be tough, but you know what we have each other. I don't remember not knowing anybody. I know that seems selfish but it's not it's just a reality. Ask anyone who's gone through what we did, and they'll say the same. I'm lucky enough to have two moms and dlys lucky to have two dads and Jim too and we're lucky to found each other and find happiness.

I got this.

As soon as I get back, I'm finally doing what my heart desired got everything out of the way I cleared all the noise out of me, and I started to write songs and perform music I have a lot of energy in me and I'm just enjoying creating in the military I started to play the guitar and that really helped me find myself. I think that is responsible for who I am. I knew when I got out of the military, I was going to move to the country capital of the world. Yes, that's right and I did. What is unknown is what the future is going to hold for me, but you know I do know one thing I'm going to be rocking it and I'm going to do for me, and I know my dad will look down. Jimmy always looked down and helped me and guide me and doing the right thing and helping me get what I want. I know he's smiling down from heaven even now give me a high five that goofy look on his face smiling proudly and I say then I salute You.

Of course, when I get back everything was different with Jen, she was performing doing her thing. She's always the best performer and the whole world she said once the reason why she liked it is because she got to escape and be someone different but no worries no sadness, she really made herself she really made something of herself, done with college and moving to LA to be somebody to make something and she will, and she will become the person I always knew. It didn't matter if we didn't have that romance anymore, I knew we'd always be close, and we are we weren't approved to end up together it's just something that helped us get through those difficult years I feel. And then talking first night back, we really bonded again, and we realized good friends and that's what we are to this day feels good oh so good. Probably write a country song about this someday, the love that wasn't meant to be. Growing up in New York you wouldn't think I would like country. But I did part because it's a story telling and the fact that you can become someone that and it just feels right you know. But it makes me feel good my favorite song is I must be wishing on someone else's Star. I found myself it was all weird. What is life going to hold for me, but I know, I do know one thing I'm going to be rocking it and I'm going to do for me, and I know my dad will look down in delight. Daddy Jimmy will always look down and help me and guide me and doing the right thing and helping me get what I want.

We weren't approved to end up together it's just something that helped us get through those difficult years I feel and then being back we really bonded again, and we realized that we would be good friends, best of friends and that's what we are to this day. It feels good oh so good.

But I found myself, so it doesn't matter. I got to leave two years in because daddy Tim was dying. He got the cancer the skin cancer from all that time in Ground Zero. I got to stay like a few months just enough time say goodbye. It was tough, I mean and only dad I knew. I know I react to all this it made me mad' cause here we go again now. I lost two people that I love from 9/11. How could God do this I don't understand.

I really don't want to run and kick in a wall I'm grateful that I had the military time. It makes me strong and pushed me. Takes away all that aggression it made me more secure, to go back to the war in which I did by the way. I did it for both my dad's. For the terrorists who took my first dad away from me and now this one. I knew mum would be OK when I left to go back, she had Jimmy and Jen and I knew they would get her through it I mean just felt bad for Jimmy' cause here he was just starting college and just graduating.Then Tim, he got the cancer the skin cancer from all that time in Ground Zero. I got to stay like a few months just enough to time say goodbye. Here we go again.

Now I lost two people that I love from 9/11. I don't understand. I'm grateful that I had the military , for both my dad's for the terrorists who took my first dad away from me and now this one a new mum would be okay ,when I left to go back she had Jimmy and Jen and I knew they would get her through it I mean just felt bad for Jimmy' cause here he was two graduating by the Tim Daddy to me, died, but he got to see him play soccer professionally which was good . Now after we buried daddy Tim, I was ready for that fresh start, and I got it. I wasn't a hero really . My daddy Tim and daddy Jimmy both are more heroes than I ever been fighting fires helping people and just being up there in the towers not making my dad my mum sad and helping people get down, he did everything he could and that taught me a lot that's the other reason why I wanted to go I want to be of service ... I know everyone says that on 9/11 everyone was helpful and for months after people were bonded coming together and I guess I just wanted that I wanted that. I got it I became of service That makes everybody happy up there now I stop and remember who I am and don't break and and I remember I don't have to be that perfect person just, But I have to say I feel the saddest for mom she lost two loves of her life, it must be hard, but she just gets out there. I'm so proud of her and will always be there for her as she is for me. And I know she has Jimmy junior still so that'll keep her going and then she'll be able to get on with things, I can't even imagine going through it twice I'm mad enough and here she is not even batting an eye. I'm just glad Jen has mommy Angela. Our mom I should say is great and we will always be a family no matter what. With angels looking out for us on all levels and I know we'll get to where we want to be. So, I rock on. I know Jimmy said Jimmy Junior says he had it worse because at least I knew dad, What would I do with the time machine. I think Jimmy didn't Junior does have one thing right you would want more and more time . I mean if I had time machine of course I'd want more time with Dad? How can I not , even though that would mean that I wouldn't be the same person that you would see before me you know now like in frequency where I can say Dad you're going to die. I love that movie where the son gets to tell his dad everything that happened in his present . They're trying to solve a crime I guess the crime I would like to solve is them getting on the plane .I would be like Dad just to go to work and come back I know there's no guarantee that we all live happily ever after if I could make anything happen maybe I'd make them divorce so I don't lose anything so I still become the writer I am today that would be great I would really like that yeah that would be the best thing to happen besides that's the reality I would choose . I don't think I need alternate realities, so it's interesting to think about what would happen or what could happen. But yeah, that movie frequency gets me every time I cry so hard that's my life. Any movie can do that that. Movies can because every boy wants a father and I'm lucky enough to have two dad's.

TIM

It sucks being sick. When the kids had to come home and take care of me and know that I was going to go or will it change anything. I don't know what I would change. I don't know what I could change. I love them all so, something that I conversate with the kids all the time. I let him know I wouldn't want to change anything but it's a very fine line. I also must let Dylan and Jimmy know that I respect the connection with their dad, and it feels weird to say that but it's like treating it like a divorce. You can't overstep your boundaries because they had a dad. They have a dad and you don't want them to think that you're replacing him especially with Dylan more so with Dylan because he remembers him his big memories, so I always had to say well I'm not trying to replace your dad he's a great guy and eventually it gets to the point where I know your dad would be proud of you and I know your dad would want me to do this .Dylan got to that point at 15 especially now he totally understands it and I know he's upset to lose someone else again heck I am too. I mean I can't believe it we work so darn hard in New York and who knew that we were killing ourselves. We did what they expected and hope they'll be compensation for everybody. They have to I mean we all know they don't have to, but it would be greatly appreciated I've worked on every bill that I could try to make this a reality especially when I knew I was getting sick I went and I tried to take care of it.I tried to give everybody what they whated.I was going to be there fair share and I guess it worked there was some kind of Bill so I'm satisfied I can let it rest once and for all. Another thing I get asked all the time is what I'd change. I'd want the kids to know they had a dad but before and after with me, but would I do anything different? I think I was a good dad and I tried to help people, I wish I could have got it sooner you know that's only one thing, I would have tried to hurry up everything but there's not much you can help hurry up you just have to let it be. Allowing the action to fall where it may be and then let him know that you're there whenever. I've done that that's what's worked that's how it's been. Which is great I'm there for the kids and they know it. I love them all the same and I couldn't be any prouder of them 100%.

As for my love for their mother, for Angela, I loved her so much, but she was going through so many hard times and all I could do is be there and I'd be doing my thing and hear about her or going to the friends of New York firefighter's thing and I would tell her about stuff. I couldn't rush the process there's no way, but I just tried to do the best for the kids no matter what as much as she let me. And overtime it became more and more. Yeah, I'm realistic to know that I wouldn't have ended up with her I mean I think Jimmy Jr's on to something about the alternate realities because I like to think there's one reality that we never got divorced.

So that even if 9/11 happened if Kathy died and Jimmy senior didn't and another one ...where ...I mean the possibilities are endless these are just the ones that I focus on in my head. The main one is just focusing on what would happen if we I didn't get to be with her. Though would I be alone. I mean I wouldn't know about this love, but

I think on some level I would have to feel it, but I know I wouldn't have tried to make them deal with me, but things are just not good that way, so my secret desire is just to be happy, and I hope they're all OK when I pass. I mean I know they know I'll be there to take care of them, and I'll be with everybody buddy and that makes them happy but who knows .I know when I passed that I will still be around I know this happened with Kathy and I know it happened too Angela too and I never once told Jim just to go away, how could I. How could I tell him go away? Kathy I could I've told her that in real life. I know I understood that Jimmy was a real part of the kid's life, I never tried to replace I was just there for them. I've walked it like a skilled type of rope Walker from the circus I know I have, and I deserve a lot of applause I'm not really saying I want that applause but ...

Being sick we have discussed it and I just said whatever I have is yours and the kids and I know she'll support Jen even though she is older now I know she's in good hands. Boy, am I mad though? I wish they would have been more honest but as Jimmy tells me really daddy you really think they would have been more honest. What will I miss the most? Going to baseball games with the kids laughing barbecuing in the summer. Just talking having those moments where you just sit and talking and have pure bliss. I think that's all that really matters.

I did get the kids blessing so to speak but I did make sure they were OK with it, and they were you know it's weird so close to death now and I just not how they must have felt that day so desperate just to jump off buildings and I feel desperate too. I'm desperate because I know there's nothing, I can do to change it we have limited amount of time, and I don't know I guess none of us really do know when our numbers up. I'm just grateful I had the time. I do know I'll miss things like walking Jen down the aisle. If she even does get married and I discussed it with Angela. I hope she gets married, and I hope they like Jen and maybe this new guy would walk her. I told Dyl you do it for me. He says he will. I know he will. As Angela says she won't remarry. I don't want her to be alone, she says don't worry I'll be fine, but I don't know.

Yeah, I'm glad I've been there for the kids I'm glad we have all this time together and of course I'd want more but none the less it is what it is and like I said my best memories are going to baseball games and all . And all those many smaller moments you take for granted. It all could all be taken away in a moment even with my cough specially with my cough. Everything was limited and yes I don't even think the kids do take anything for granted they knew especially Dylan and Jen they knew. Jimmy, I guess even he knows, how can he not be growing up in the shadow of 9/11. That's the one thing that bonds this whole community that no one else understands. I think is that we all know this can be taken away in a moment. Time does stand still. It is not like you're preparing any one . You just know how beautiful it is to have what you have and what I'd give for one more kiss or just one more peaceful Firefly summer night and the trip to the beach or the theme park or ball park. Even the bad times with Dylan yelling at me or just looking at me like I'm a doofus or fight with Angela. I would take any of that just one more time. Honestly I would , I know I sound like a character from our town but it's true those small moments good and bad and I guess being a firefighter I always knew that I never took anything for granted' cause I knew I could be gone like that, like in the snap of a finger, it all could just be taken away. So I knew that before 9/ 11 too and now I know it even more It's always that reality.

ANGELA

Don't get me started when I think of losing Tim I cry. Here I am all over again and I mean it. I don't think I would ever have lost anyone again.

I don't think I'd ever want to have lost another husband I don't think I can bear to be remarried and I mean that when I told him that there's no one else I would marry. I never ...maybe a companion but then I'll have the grandkids for that someday look at me they're only twenty. Maybe I'll find someone to just go to the movies with. Never say never because I never thought I'd be married again twice, so you never know, life is full of those surprises it really is.

In terms of a time machine like Jimmy talks about yeah, I guess I want a time machine. Honestly,

I think, I had more to tend to. I believe in the alternate realities. I mean yeah, I'd want to not lose Jimmy, but then I could imagine not knowing Tim or at least knowing him but in another capacity. So that's why I say I know I would know no difference if I had lost. If I went back in time and there's no guarantees that me and Jimmy would have stayed together. Though I can't see what would have broken us up but then I would have never seen 9/11 either so just goes to show, you never know. That's what I appreciate the most now live each day to the fullest one day at a time. It took me forever to realize that and have those models in my head now . I was so sad for so long, I wasted so much time. So much precious time but I get it now. I miss him, his smiles the way he just reads the paper and watches the news. He's a total opposite of Jimmy senior. But at the same time both providers. Both give you what you need and that's the truth. I'm glad how Jimmy wasn't too extreme, and Tim wasn't too bold and too scary he didn't expect things he just let things happen but at the same time he was there. After all this, for the kids and there for me. Most importantly for the kids . Like a great dad really is. I know Jimmy in a weird way would have liked him ,he would have.

He's always there for me I always see him and he's told me that the kids um are lucky you're lucky he gave me his approval and pushed me into it. Not that I wouldn't have anyway but it helps to know it's approved and I know all that seems weird but it's true and with Tim's death I was prepared and it scared me but I know I'd have support. I knew I'd have support and I was right everyone was there everyone understood and felt my pain. So I'm never alone especially on 9/11 itself but even in between ,I got friends.I mean it was slow how I fell in love with them we were just good friends hanging out and I said I never planned it at all we were just really good friends and we each had each other and he got me through the rough patches. When Jimmy was first born I couldn't do anything and he was the reason why I got out of bed he would say you have a kid to raise and he wouldn't let me just stop life. He knew how important it was and that perspective really helped me, guide me into it and for that I'm ever grateful. Not to be weird but this time at least I had a body I now have a funeral to go to and I'm prepared for it but I know what's happening this time around and I'm glad that I have an actual place to go to I know that seems like a weird thing to be grateful for but with Jimmy I just have a mountain and a wall with a name and there wasn't enough parts of him .We did Bury some of his some of his stuff and that was nice but it's not the same. I know it sounds perverse but you don't understand unless you've been through it .How important is to get that closure. I get how important it is to say everything you'd want to say and of course there's always more conversations, that never happened more talks and more walks and more holidays never the perfect time but at least I got closure. I got to tell him how much I loved him and thank you and all that and the kids got closure and we knew it was happening. Oh that was for real and not in my head or pretending that it happened, I got real closure.You are never prepared though regardless. You can't be prepared but you can get closure and I think that's important, the most important thing. I see him too I see Tim too, he is with me, sometimes I see them together

Tim and Jimmy laughing and talking, they are there for each other or show up at the same time, that can be awkward but at least most of the time it's separate and sometimes I'll tell him leave but then I sit here at the 9/11 memorial I should have been silent and wait. I listen for the bells to tell for those we lost. I'm listening for the bells reminding us of when and where we were twenty years ago. Internally I'm crying and externally I try to be sad but not too sad to find the balance because I know if I cry, I'll cry and never let go if that's possible. I'm thinking about everything when I look back now that it's been twenty years and we've lost him. I lost my dad I'm glad to have Angela. But Dylan in terms of The Time Machine. I mean my parents we're going to divorced anyway but course I'd want more time with Mama Kathy, and I think what I would do is sleep. Probably just fake sick ,so she didn't have to go in or like Dly said just make it so they never got on the plane and trick him back and hoped and maybe in that reality, Dylan and I would have gotten married there would be no brokenness but of course I'd still be broken cause the divorce and maybe Dylan would be too maybe in his parents would have gotten divorced even though they were the cleavers but regardless I guess I would hope that Dylan and I would get married. I mean I'm glad that he's there for me now and is my best friend that's almost better but I just wonder what that reality would look like' cause as it is I can't imagine getting married to anyone that means no grandkids maybe Dylan will but I guess Jimmy is his best moms best bet . We do need someone junior sorry hoping you will have at least one kid that would be nice to add to our family . I'm becoming an activist that's why I'm trying to fight for my family. If I hadn't been an actress I would have been a lawyer but I like disappearing into other people's perfect world and sometimes not so perfect but when you're little you get to be someone else and you get to create their story and say yeah it is perfect at least it's not mine at least it's not my story. Yeah I'll miss my dad but I'm mad too I think I had an easier time growing up than some just knowing that my parents were going to get divorced according to Dad but I know he wouldn't lie to me.

The dead are part of our lives they walk amongst us and for that I am grateful so now they're never really gone truly.

JeN

Now Daddy's gone he took his last breath and I try not to cry too hard. Yet another chapter done and another is about to begin. I don't even want to think about the funeral of the burying. None of that stuff it's too hard to think about it's all too fresh. There's plenty of time I love my papa. For now we sit in a circle and we hug each other and remember what a good guy he was what a good dad and husband to Mommy. I still want to slap someone and ask why but I know he wants us to be strong and so I am I'm strong for Daddy and I look at Tim, Jimmy Jr , mama Angela and Dly and I know they're thinking the same thing we must be strong. We must we must. So that's what he would have wanted.

Dad did not make it to the twenty years he died one year sooner. I don't know what to think I remember when Angela called me and then I had to call Dylan and Jimmy she was so devastated she said dad was sick come home and I cried and cried. He had the lung disease I guess he got it he didn't smoke it anything at all I guess he got it from all the debris on 9/11 he was there for months afterwards cleaning up the rebel looking for people looking for Mom looking for Jimmy trying to find himself too I guess as he says. Took him too just in a different way. As I sit and watch the news, I get scared it gets sad. Those who lived it know what it's like and worry if it would happen again, it's like PTSD in the brain, I was only seven ,now 20 years later I'm 27 and I'm scared. I'm a filmmaker now I make films and document things and make people laugh.I think that started a long time ago ,I had my camera all the time with me just to see so I'd remember.I finally get I think I was scared that I would forget so I took my camera everywhere I went. On that day I remember my mom took me to school I was too young to know but I guess no one really knew what was going on I was going to say I was too young to know what was really going on and of course I didn't know it was the last time I would see my mom I was just naive kid but we all were . It's a day that changed everything, when I close my eyes I see her walking away and I want to scream no mommy come back but I don't and she doesn't and I walk on to school like it was any other day because who knew it wasn't going to be it was the end of something in the beginning of something new he's always beginnings and endings and they're usually not as clear but this one was. I didn't know Dylan ,back then he was just another kid in school . I mean we were from Brooklyn which was just a small community. He was just a popular kid, can you be popular at 7 but he was. Like I said I really didn't know him I knew of him. I didn't know his mom either.My dad was a firefighter from 9/11 he was a great firefighter he did everything he could to protect those that day and ultimately, he got sick because of it but if the price you pay for being a hero and my dad he was a hero, he was I know all girls say that about their daddies but to me he was . I had to share him. I miss you daddy I cry, and I think of you everyday.

DYLAN

How hard is it to say goodbye. When you don't want to say goodbye. I hope you never have to find out it's the hardest thing in the world I will tell you that I sit and I cry and I hug my family and feel very alone. I know Dad said to think of the next chapter what you're going to do and I will but for now I have to cry and later I'll be able to make a song out of it, but for now all I can do is cry and I know when I look at them they all feel the same.

JIMMY JR

I can't believe dad took his last breath it's impossible. I look at him and realize it's true I want to run out of the room but I don't I stand strong. I'm just more in the loss of words in the loss of such a great man. A great dad one that gave everything we truly needed.

ANGELA

I don't want the kids to see my tears but I know they know and there's nothing to be ashamed of. And so I let it flow we all don't say a word but I know we feel the memories and we feel the loss of something great and for me I know I owe him my second life. It is going to be harder than I thought to rebuild who I am, and to rebuild who I'm going to be. I know I can do it and I know he'll be my guardian angel watching over me just like Jimmy and now I have two guardian angels and it helps me to know that Dylan will write the story and put all the stories out there. Maybe he or Jen will even make a documentary about it and I smile to know Tim's spirit will live on. I'll make sure his name gets up on the wall even though he didn't die and on that September Day. I will fight hard to make that happen. We will never forget that, I will never forget the love of my life. I know Jimmy senior is looking out for him waiting for him, to take him to the other side. I feel Jimmy's presence too for the first time in a long time and I know my guys are together.I smile at that. And all this it is so comforting to know that, just thinking of them helping each other is the only thing that can bring a smile to my face. Just knowing they're together brings me peace.

TIM

As I took my last breath my kids were all around me. And above me I see Jimmy Sr . I Tell my kids I see your daddy Jimmy . All I remember is them crying and saying no Daddy Angeles smiled at me and whispered is he happy or sad or mad and I said he's happy well not happy and necessarily but he's not mad at me and she smiled that's good he's there for you and I nodded.

It's not your time the kids all said. I was able to get out in a whisper that I love them and that I was glad to have all the years I was glad that we became a family. They held my hands tight and I held their hands, I took my last breath. Ready but I wasn't ready but I knew it was my time and I took his hand. They were all waiting for me Kathy and Jimmy. The new I wasn't ready but whoever is and I saw them staring at me crying. Both told me it was going to be okay and I knew I would watch over them forever.

JEN

Now on the September Day I stare at the Blue sky and say goodbye. Daddy Tim goodbye , goodbye mommy Kathy .I'm just trying not to cry. I wish I knew what to say to you. I didn't know it should not be so hard. Daddy I'm sorry you'll never get to walk me down the aisle and see your grandkids. I wish I could just have one more laugh with you, I would take it but I know that wouldn't be enough and Mommy Kathy you know what I want I want a time machine but I would miss Angela. You'd be proud of who I became Mommy I know you would your little girls grown up now. Thank you for giving me the foundation for who I would become. For that I love you to the Moon and back and I think of you everyday, now I say good night not goodbye good night. my time is here is not done. No I will see you someday take care of daddy until I get there to Angela gets there. Bye for now.

DYLAN

Goodbye daddy Tim. I wish I had more time with you I really do thanks for making the man out of me. Daddy Jimmy you know I wish I had more time with you I don't know what to say. I don't know what to say to either one of you thanks seems too little. I can't say goodbye I know you'll be with me forever and then I'll see you someday so I'll say in general see you later. I guess I just want to thank you and Daddy Tim for giving me the ability to be who I am and to love and I'm forever grateful that I look in the mirror and I can see a little bit of you and that reminds me of you.I will never forget you even though I had you such a little time , you're with me in here in my heart and Tim thank you. You know what you mean to me I'll never forget all the nights we talked and all you gave to me thanks for being there for me when I needed to talk and when I pushed you away. Thanks for filling in for for Daddy Jim even though all I wanted was him you knew and you waited and finally it's you I wanted. I still want . I know how long it's going to take for me to get over this but I love you and I know you know I hope you know that. So I'm just going to say ciao.

JIMMY Jr

Goodbye dad's. Both I knew too little and one not at all. But I want to thank you both for giving me the ability to love and to laugh and to be strong. Thank you I will take that into everything I do from now until the last breath I take. I know everyone says I look like you Daddy Jim and I guess I do I want to see that even though sometimes I think I look like you Tim and I know that's not possible but they do say pets begin to look like their owners and that's not possible so maybe a little of you got into me Daddy Tim that's all I wanted to say that's all I can say thanks so much. Took me so long to love you Daddy Tim because you are all I had I never held back like Dylan but I just want to say thanks for being my rock and and daddy Jim thank you for the gens and I really do mean if I had a time machine I'd go back just so I could meet you. Farewell angels.

ANGELA

I don't know how to do this , I thought I could do it. Thank you to my two soulmates I never thought I could love again but I did and I will continue to love you guys forever . I seriously doubt I'll find a third just to let you know but I didn't think I'd find a second but I really don't think I'll find it there. Tim darling you are my soulmate I just want to let you know my high school college best friend not a day goes by I don't think of you and even though I'm married again to my dear sweet Tim I'm glad I could give him the love and then he could love me back and that we made a family so take care of him up there Jimmy until we meet again guys I can't wait. You both are my heroes.

epilogue

I just ask everyone to remember the people who gave their lives in the last 20 plus years for all this to happen and pray for all the families affected and praying that nothing more happens. I don't want my Dad's life to be in vain. Their life's cannot be in vain. All I ask is for prays and oh and for everyone to remember those that left us to soon . Never forget. I won't .

Whenever I hear a fire truck, I think of Papa Tim. He would watch the news every night at the end. He would always say where's he fires. There's storm chasers and fire chasers. Papa Tim was a fire chaser. He knows where all the fires were and all the details.

He would sit in the bed at the end, and I would sit next to him and smile up at him as he talked with such passion about the fires. I couldn't help but feel the same passion and I would research with him where the fire was. Was it uptown or down or witch captain was fighting the fire and why he was the best for the job? That's papa Tim. Mom would smile and watch us. Losing papa Tim was hard. I think harder even that day. Tim was a victim of 9/11 too, like us all, but he got the lung cancer from fighting after. All those long months. I never knew my dad Jimmy, but I had 20 years with Tim. He fought it longer than most because he had that will to live and didn't want to let us down but in the end 9/11 took him like it takes the rest of us every day. It's something you never forget.

I think of this as I hear them call Jimmy's name and Kathy's and now Tim's

It's all done I fade out. I will always be there for them always watching over my babies the one I knew and the one that I didn't and my wife too. I look at them with crying eyes for everything they've gone through I've watched my babies grow up and watch my wife move on. I would have wanted it all if it all had been reversed. I of course would have wanted to move on, and I know she would have wanted me to, but I drop her signs all the time, so she knows that I love her, that it's okay to move on and I sit here on the anniversary with all the other spirits and souls of those lost,. All of us will need to find peace for our families. I know it's hard and I know it's worth it .I wish there was a time machine that I could go back in time and tell them all that I love them and not go to work and maybe have just one last meal with them and so I can get one last hug, that would be nice. Who wouldn't choose another reality. Oh how I wish I could. But I am glad that I saved everybody and I'm glad for those that got to live. I did my duty for that I'm proud.

This is the last time, so I sprinkle dust and see a flash in Angela's eyes, and I know she saw, that she knows. I blow kisses and I fade out. I let Tim take my hand as I guide him to the other side.

As the sound of fire trunks howl from the distance one last time.